Marionettes, Inc.

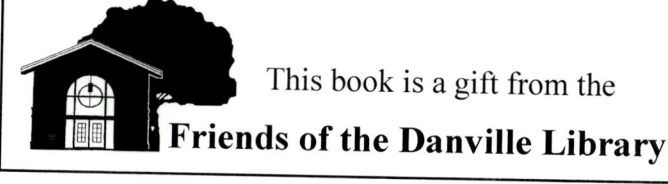
This book is a gift from the
Friends of the Danville Library

Marionettes, Inc.

Ray Bradbury

Subterranean Press 2009

Marionettes, Inc. Copyright © 2009 by Ray Bradbury. All rights reserved.

Endsheet image © 2009 by Ray Bradbury. All rights reserved.

Dust jacket and interior illustrations Copyright © 2009 by Mark A. Nelson. All rights reserved.

Interior design Copyright © 2009 by Desert Isle Design, LLC. All rights reserved.

"I Sing the Body Electric" Copyright © 1969, renewed 1977 by Ray Bradbury.
"Marionettes, Inc." Copyright © 1949 by Better Publications, renewed 1976 by Ray Bradbury.
"Changeling" Copyright © 1949 by Better Publications, renewed 1976 by Ray Bradbury.
"Punishment Without Crime" Copyright © 1950 by Clark Publishing, renewed 1977 by Ray Bradbury.
"Wind-up World" Copyright © 2009 by Ray Bradbury. Appears here for the first time.
"Murder by Facsimile" Copyright © 2009 by Ray Bradbury. Appears here for the first time.

First Edition

ISBN
978-1-59606-215-3

Subterranean Press
PO Box 190106
Burton, MI 48519

www.subterraneanpress.com

The publisher would like to thank Donn Albright for his sleuthing skills in finding the rarities for this volume, and his invaluable aid in putting it together.

Table of Contents

I Sing the Body Electric 7

Marionettes, Inc. 65

Changeling 79

Punishment Without Crime 93

Wind-up World 109

Murder by Facsimile 113

I SING THE BODY ELECTRIC

Grandma!

I remember her birth.

Wait, you say, *no* man remembers his own grandma's birth.

But, yes, *we* remember the day that she was born.

For we, her grandchildren, slapped her to life. Timothy, Agatha, and I, Tom, raised up our hands and brought them down in a huge crack! We shook together the bits and pieces, parts and samples, textures and tastes, humors and distillations that would move her compass needle north to cool us, south to warm and comfort us, east and west to travel round the endless world, glide her eyes to know us, mouth to sing us asleep by night, hands to touch us awake at dawn.

Grandma, O dear and wondrous electric dream...

When storm lightnings rove the sky making circuitries amidst the clouds, her name flashes on my inner lid. Sometimes still I hear her ticking, humming above our beds in the gentle dark. She passes like a clock-ghost in the long halls of memory, like a hive of intellectual bees swarming after the Spirit of Summers Lost. Sometimes still I feel the smile I learned from her, printed on my cheek at three in the deep morn...

All right, all right! you cry, what was it like the day your damned and wondrous-dreadful-loving Grandma was born?

It was the week the world ended...

• • •

Our mother was dead.

One late afternoon a black car left Father and the three of us stranded on our own front drive staring at the grass, thinking:

That's not our grass. There are the croquet mallets, balls, hoops, yes, just as they fell and lay three days ago when Dad stumbled out on the lawn, weeping with the news. There are the roller skates that belonged to a boy, me, who will never be that young again. And yes, there the tire-swing on the old oak, but Agatha afraid to swing. It would surely break. It would fall.

And the house? Oh, God...

We peered through the front door, afraid of the echoes we might find confused in the halls; the sort of clamor that happens when all the furniture is taken out and there is nothing to soften the river of talk that flows in any house at all hours. And now the soft, the warm, the main piece of lovely furniture was gone forever.

The door drifted wide.

Silence came out. Somewhere a cellar door stood wide and a raw wind blew damp earth from under the house.

But, I thought, we don't *have* a cellar!

"Well," said Father.

We did not move.

Aunt Clara drove up the path in her big canary-colored limousine.

We jumped through the door. We ran to our rooms.

• • •

We heard them shout and then speak and then shout and then speak: Let the children live with me! Aunt Clara said. They'd rather kill themselves! Father said.

A door slammed. Aunt Clara was gone.

We almost danced. Then we remembered what had happened and went downstairs.

Father sat alone talking to himself or to a remnant ghost of Mother left from the days before her illness, but jarred loose now by the slamming of the door. He murmured to his hands, his empty palms:

"The children need someone. I love them but, let's face it, I must work to feed us all. You love them, Ann, but you're gone. And Clara? Impossible. She loves but smothers. And as for maids, nurses—?"

Here Father sighed and we sighed with him, remembering.

The luck we had had with maids or live-in teachers or sitters was beyond intolerable. Hardly a one who wasn't a crosscut saw grabbing against the grain. Handaxes and hurricanes best described them. Or, conversely, they were all fallen trifle, damp soufflé. We children were unseen furniture to be sat upon or dusted or sent for reupholstering come spring and fall, with a yearly cleansing at the beach.

"What we need," said Father, "is a…"

We all leaned to his whisper.

"…grandmother."

"But," said Timothy, with the logic of nine years, "all our grandmothers are dead."

"Yes in one way, no in another."

What a fine mysterious thing for Dad to say.

"Here," he said at last.

He handed us a multifold, multicolored pamphlet. We had seen it in his hands, off and on, for many weeks, and very often during the last few days. Now, with one blink of our eyes, as we passed the paper from hand to hand, we knew why Aunt Clara, insulted, outraged, had stormed from the house.

Timothy was the first to read aloud from what he saw on the first page:

"I Sing the Body Electric!"

He glanced up at Father, squinting. "What the heck does that mean?"

"Read on."

Agatha and I glanced guiltily about the room, afraid Mother might suddenly come in to find us with this blasphemy, but then nodded to Timothy, who read:

"'Fanto—'"

"Fantoccini," Father prompted.

"'Fantoccini Ltd. We *Shadow Forth*...the answer to all your most grievous problems. One Model Only, upon which a thousand times a thousand variations can be added, subtracted, subdivided, indivisible, with Liberty and Justice for all.'"

"Where does it say *that?*" we all cried.

"It doesn't." Timothy smiled for the first time in days. "I just had to put that in. Wait." He read on: "'for you who have worried over inattentive sitters, nurses who cannot be trusted with marked liquor bottles, and well-meaning Uncles and Aunts—'"

"Well-meaning, *but!*" said Agatha, and I gave an echo.

"'—we have perfected the first humanoid-genre mini-circuited, rechargeable AC-DC Mark V Electrical Grandmother…'"

"Grandmother!?"

The paper slipped away to the floor. "Dad…?"

"Don't look at me that way," said Father. "I'm half-mad with grief, and half-mad thinking of tomorrow and the day after that. Someone pick up the paper. Finish it."

"I will," I said, and did:

"'The Toy that is more than a Toy, the Fantoccini Electrical Grandmother is built with loving precision to give the incredible precision of love to your children. The child at ease with the realities of the world and the even greater realities of the imagination, is her aim.

"'She is computerized to tutor in twelve languages simultaneously, capable of switching tongues in a thousandth of a second without pause, and has a complete knowledge of the religious, artistic, and sociopolitical histories of the world seeded in her master hive—'"

"How great!" said Timothy. "It makes it sound as if we were to keep bees! *Educated* bees!"

"Shut up!" said Agatha.

"'Above all,'" I read, "'this human being, for human she seems, this embodiment in electro-intelligent facsimile of the humanities, will listen, know, tell, react and love your children insofar as such great Objects, such fantastic Toys, can be said to Love, or can be imagined to Care. This Miraculous Companion, excited to the challenge of large world and small, inner Sea or Outer Universe, will transmit by touch and tell, said Miracles to your Needy.'"

"Our Needy," murmured Agatha.

Why, we all thought, sadly, that's us, oh, yes, that's *us*.

I finished:

"'We do not sell our Creation to able-bodied families where parents are available to raise, effect, shape, change, love their own children. Nothing can replace the parent in the home. However there are families where death or ill health or disablement undermines the welfare of the children. Orphanages seem not the answer. Nurses tend to be selfish, neglectful, or suffering from dire nervous afflictions.

"'With the utmost humility then, and recognizing the need to rebuild, rethink, and regrow our conceptualizations from month to month, year to year, we offer the nearest thing to the Ideal Teacher-Friend-Companion-Blood Relation. A trial period can be arranged for—'"

"Stop," said Father. "Don't go on. Even I can't stand it."

"Why?" said Timothy. "I was just getting interested."

I folded the pamphlet up. "Do they *really* have these things?"

"Let's not talk any more about it," said Father, his hand over his eyes. "It was a mad thought—"

"Not so mad," I said, glancing at Tim. "I mean, heck, even if they tried, whatever they built, couldn't be worse than Aunt Clara, huh?"

And then we all roared. We hadn't laughed in months. And now my simple words made everyone hoot and howl and explode. I opened my mouth and yelled happily, too.

When we stopped laughing, we looked at the pamphlet and I said, "Well?"

"I—" Agatha scowled, not ready.

"We do need something, bad, right now," said Timothy.

"I have an open mind," I said, in my best pontifical style.

"There's only one thing," said Agatha. "We can try it. Sure."

"But—tell me this—when do we cut out all this talk and when does our *real* mother come home to stay?"

There was a single gasp from the family as if, with one shot, she had struck us all in the heart.

I don't think any of us stopped crying the rest of that night.

• • •

I SING THE BODY ELECTRIC

It was a clear bright day. The helicopter tossed us lightly up and over and down through the skyscrapers and let us out, almost for a trot and caper, on top of the building where the large letters could be read from the sky:

FANTOCCINI.

"What are *Fantoccini?*" said Agatha.

"It's an Italian word for shadow puppets, I think, or dream people," said Father.

"But *shadow forth,* what does that mean?"

"WE TRY TO GUESS YOUR DREAM," I said.

"Bravo," said Father. "A-Plus."

I beamed.

The helicopter flapped a lot of loud shadows over us and went away.

We sank down in an elevator as our stomachs sank up. We stepped out onto a moving carpet that streamed away on a blue river of wool toward a desk over which various signs hung:

THE CLOCK SHOP
Fantoccini Our Specialty.
Rabbits on walls, no problem.

"Rabbits on walls?"

I held up my fingers in profile as if I held them before a candle flame, and wiggled the "ears."

"Here's a rabbit, here's a wolf, here's a crocodile."

"Of course," said Agatha.

And we were at the desk. Quiet music drifted about us. Somewhere behind the walls, there was a waterfall of machinery flowing softly. As we arrived at the desk, the lighting changed to make us look warmer, happier, though we were still cold.

All about us in niches and cases, and hung from ceilings on wires and strings were puppets and marionettes, and Balinese kite-bamboo-translucent dolls which, held to the moonlight, might acrobat your most secret nightmares or dreams. In passing, the breeze set up by our bodies stirred the various hung souls on their gibbets. It was like an immense lynching on a holiday at some English crossroads four hundred years before.

You see? I know my history.

Agatha blinked about with disbelief and then some touch of awe and finally disgust.

"Well, if that's what they are, let's go."

"Tush," said Father.

"Well," she protested, "you gave me one of those dumb things with strings two years ago and the strings were in a zillion knots by dinnertime. I threw the whole thing out the window."

"Patience," said Father.

"We shall see what we can do to eliminate the strings."

The man behind the desk had spoken.

We all turned to give him our regard.

Rather like a funeral-parlor man, he had the cleverness not to smile. Children are put off by older people who smile too much. They smell a catch, right off.

Unsmiling, but not gloomy or pontifical, the man said, "Guido Fantoccini, at your service. Here's how we do it, Miss Agatha Simmons, aged eleven."

Now there was a really fine touch.

He knew that Agatha was only ten. Add a year to that, and you're halfway home. Agatha grew an inch. The man went on:

"There."

And he placed a golden key in Agatha's hand.

"To wind them up instead of strings?"

"To wind them up." The man nodded.

"Pshaw!" said Agatha.

Which was her polite form of "rabbit pellets."

"God's truth. Here is the key to your Do-it-Yourself, Select Only the Best, Electrical Grandmother. Every morning you wind her up. Every night you let her run down. You're in charge. You are guardian of the Key."

He pressed the object in her palm where she looked at it suspiciously.

I watched him. He gave me a side wink which said, well, no…but aren't keys fun?

I winked back before she lifted her head.

"Where does this fit?"

"You'll see when the time comes. In the middle of her stomach, perhaps, or up her left nostril or in her right ear."

That was good for a smile as the man arose.

"This way, please. Step light. Onto the moving stream. Walk on the water, please. Yes. There."

He helped to float us. We stepped from rug that was forever frozen onto rug that whispered by.

It was a most agreeable river which floated us along on a green spread of carpeting that rolled forever through halls and into wonderfully secret dim caverns where voices echoed back our own breathing or sang like Oracles to our questions.

"Listen," said the salesman, "the voices of all kinds of women. Weigh and find just the right one…!"

And listen we did, to all the high, low, soft, loud, in-between, half-scolding, half-affectionate voices saved over from times before we were born.

And behind us, Agatha tread backward, always fighting the river, never catching up, never with us, holding off.

"Speak," said the salesman. "Yell."

And speak and yell we did.

"Hello. You there! This is Timothy, hi!"

"What shall I say!" I shouted. "Help!"

Agatha walked backward, mouth tight.

Father took her hand. She cried out.

"Let go! No, no! I won't have my voice used! I won't!"

"Excellent." The salesman touched three dials on a small machine he held in his hand.

On the side of the small machine we saw three oscillograph patterns mix, blend, and repeat our cries.

The salesman touched another dial and we heard our voices fly off amidst the Delphic caves to hang upside down, to cluster, to beat words all about, to shriek, and the salesman itched another knob to add, perhaps, a touch of this or a pinch of that, a breath of mother's voice, all unbeknownst, or a splice of father's outrage at the morning's paper or his peaceable one-drink voice at dusk. Whatever it was the salesman did, whispers danced all about us like frantic vinegar gnats, fizzed by lightning, settling round until at last a final switch was pushed and a voice spoke free of a far electronic deep:

"Nefertiti," it said.

Timothy froze. I froze. Agatha stopped treading water.

"Nefertiti?" asked Tim.

"What does that mean?" demanded Agatha.

"I know."

The salesman nodded me to tell.

"Nefertiti," I whispered, "is Egyptian for The Beautiful One Is Here."

"The Beautiful One Is Here," repeated Timothy.

"Nefer," said Agatha, "titi."

And we all turned to stare into that soft twilight, that deep far place from which the good warm soft voice came.

And she was indeed there.

And, by her voice, she was beautiful…

• • •

That was it.

That was, at least, the most of it.

The voice seemed more important than all the rest.

Not that we didn't argue about weights and measures:

She should not be bony to cut us to the quick, nor so fat we might sink out of sight when she squeezed us.

Her hand pressed to ours, or brushing our brow in the middle of sick-fever nights, must not be marble-cold, dreadful, or oven-hot, oppressive, but somewhere between. The nice temperature of a baby chick held in the hand after a long night's sleep and just plucked from beneath a contemplative hen; that, that was it.

Oh, we were great ones for detail. We fought and argued and cried, and Timothy won on the color of her eyes, for reasons to be known later.

Grandmother's hair? Agatha, with girl's ideas, though reluctantly given, she was in charge of that. We let her choose from a thousand harp strands hung in filamentary tapestries like varieties of rain we ran amongst. Agatha did not run happily, but seeing we boys would mess things in tangles, she told us to move aside.

And so the bargain shopping through the dime-store inventories and the Tiffany extensions of the Ben Franklin Electric Storm Machine and Fantoccini Pantomime Company was done.

And the always flowing river ran its tide to an end and deposited us all on a far shore in the late day...

• • •

It was very clever of the Fantoccini people, after that.

How?

They made us wait.

They knew we were not won over. Not completely, no, nor half completely.

Especially Agatha, who turned her face to her wall and saw sorrow there and put her hand out again and again to touch it. We found her fingernail marks on the wallpaper each morning, in strange little silhouettes, half beauty, half nightmare. Some could be erased with a breath, like ice flowers on a winter pane. Some could not be rubbed out with a washcloth, no matter how hard you tried.

And meanwhile, they made us wait.

So we fretted out June.

So we sat around July.

So we groused through August and then on August 29, "I have this feeling," said Timothy, and we all went out after breakfast to sit on the lawn.

Perhaps we had smelled something on Father's conversation the previous night or caught some special furtive glance at the sky or the freeway. Rapped briefly and then lost in his gaze. Or perhaps it was merely the way the wind blew the ghost curtains out over our beds, making pale messages all night.

For suddenly there we were in the middle of the grass, Timothy and I, with Agatha, pretending no curiosity, up on the porch, hidden behind the potted geraniums.

We gave her no notice. We knew that if we acknowledged her presence, she would flee, so we sat and watched the sky where nothing moved but birds and highflown jets, and watched the freeway where a thousand cars might suddenly deliver forth our Special Gift...but...nothing.

At noon we chewed grass and lay low...

At one o'clock, Timothy blinked his eyes.

And then, with incredible precision, it happened.

It was as if the Fantoccini people knew our surface tension.

All children are water-striders. We skate along the top skin of the pond each day, always threatening to break through, sink, vanish beyond recall, into ourselves.

Well, as if knowing our long wait must absolutely end within one minute! this *second!* no more, God, forget it!

At that instant, I repeat, the clouds above our house opened wide and let forth a helicopter like Apollo driving his chariot across mythological skies.

And the Apollo machine swam down on its own summer breeze, wafting hot winds to cool, reweaving our hair, smartening our eyebrows, applauding our pant legs against our shins, making a flag of Agatha's hair on the porch and thus settled like a vast frenzied hibiscus on our lawn, the helicopter slid wide a bottom drawer and deposited upon the grass a parcel of largish size, no sooner having laid same than the vehicle, with not so much as a god bless or farewell, sank straight up, disturbed the calm air with a mad ten thousand flourishes and then, like a skyborne dervish, tilted and fell off to be mad some other place.

Timothy and I stood riven for a long moment looking at the packing case, and then we saw the crowbar taped to the top of the raw pine lid and seized it and began to pry and creak and squeal the boards off, one by one, and as we did this I saw Agatha sneak up to watch and I thought, thank you, God, thank you that Agatha never saw a coffin, when Mother went away, no box, no cemetery, no earth, just words in a big church, no box, no box like *this*…!

The last pine plank fell away.

Timothy and I gasped. Agatha, between us now, gasped, too.

For inside the immense raw pine package was the most beautiful idea anyone ever dreamt and built.

Inside was the perfect gift for any child from seven to seventy-seven.

We stopped up our breaths. We let them out in cries of delight and adoration.

Inside the opened box was…

A mummy.

Or, first anyway, a mummy case, a sarcophagus!

"Oh, no!" Happy tears filled Timothy's eyes.

"It can't be!" said Agatha.

"It is, it is!"

"Our very own?"

"Ours !"

"It must be a mistake!"

"Sure, they'll want it back!"

"They can't *have* it!"

"Lord, Lord, is that real gold!? Real hieroglyphs! Run your fingers over them!"

"Let *me!*"

"Just like in the museums! Museums!"

We all gabbled at once. I think some tears fell from my own eyes to rain upon the case.

"Oh, they'll make the colors run!"

Agatha wiped the rain away.

And the golden mask face of the woman carved on the sarcophagus lid looked back at us with just the merest smile which hinted at our own joy, which accepted the overwhelming upsurge of a love we thought had drowned forever but now surfaced into the sun.

Not only did she have a sun-metal face stamped and beaten out of purest gold, with delicate nostrils and a mouth that was both firm and gentle, but her eyes fixed into their sockets, were cerulean or amethystine or lapus lazuli, or all three, minted and fused together, and her body was covered over with lions and eyes and ravens, and her hands were crossed upon her carved bosom and in one gold mitten she clenched a thonged whip for obedience, and in the other a fantastic ranuncula, which makes for obedience out of love, so the whip lies unused…

And as our eyes ran down her hieroglyphs it came to all three of us at the same instant:

"Why, those signs!" "Yes, the hen tracks!" "The birds, the snakes!"

They didn't speak tales of the Past.

They were hieroglyphs of the Future.

This was the first queen mummy delivered forth in all time whose papyrus inkings etched out the next month, the next season, the next year, the next *lifetime!*

She did not mourn for time spent.

No. She celebrated the bright coinage yet to come, banked, waiting, ready to be drawn upon and used.

We sank to our knees to worship that possible time.

First one hand, then another, probed out to niggle, twitch, touch, itch over the signs.

"There's me, yes, look! Me, in sixth grade!" said Agatha, now in the fifth. "See the girl with my-colored hair and wearing my gingerbread suit?"

"There's me in the twelfth year of high school!" said Timothy, so very young now but building taller stilts every week and stalking around the yard.

"There's me," I said, quietly, warm, "in college. The guy wearing glasses who runs a little to fat. Sure. Heck." I snorted. "That's me."

The sarcophagus spelled winters ahead, springs to squander, autumns to spend with all the golden and rusty and copper leaves like coins, and over all, her bright sun symbol, daughter-of-Ra eternal face, forever above our horizon, forever an illumination to tilt our shadows to better ends.

"Hey!" we all said at once, having read and reread our Fortune-Told scribblings, seeing our lifelines and lovelines, inadmissible, serpentined over, around, and down. "Hey!"

And in one séance table-lifting feat, not telling each other what to do, just doing it, we pried up the bright sarcophagus lid, which had no hinges but lifted out like cup from cup, and put the lid aside.

And within the sarcophagus, of course, was the true mummy!

And she was like the image carved on the lid, but more so, more beautiful, more touching because human shaped, and shrouded all in new fresh bandages of linen, round and round, instead of old and dusty cerements.

And upon her hidden face was an identical golden mask, younger than the first, but somehow, strangely wiser than the first.

And the linens that tethered her limbs had symbols on them of three sorts, one a girl of ten, one a boy of nine, one a boy of thirteen.

A series of bandages for each of us!

We gave each other a startled glance and a sudden bark of laughter.

Nobody said the bad joke, but all thought:

She's all wrapped up in us!

And we didn't care. We loved the joke. We loved whoever had thought to make us part of the ceremony we now went through as each of us seized and began to unwind each of his or her particular serpentines of delicious stuffs!

The lawn was soon a mountain of linen.

The woman beneath the covering lay there, waiting.

"Oh, no," cried Agatha. "She's dead, too!"

She ran. I stopped her. "Idiot. She's not dead *or* alive. Where's your key?"

"Key?"

"Dummy," said Tim, "the key the man gave you to wind her up!" Her hand had already spidered along her blouse to where the symbol of some possible new religion hung. She had strung it there, against her own skeptic's muttering, and now she held it in her sweaty palm.

"Go on," said Timothy. "Put it in!"

"But *where?*"

"Oh for God's sake! As the man said, in her right armpit or left ear. Gimme!"

And he grabbed the key and impulsively moaning with impatience and not able to find the proper insertion slot, prowled over the prone figure's head and bosom and at last, on pure instinct, perhaps for a lark, perhaps just giving up the whole damned mess, thrust the key through a final shroud of bandage at the navel.

On the instant: *spunnng!*

The Electrical Grandmother's eyes flicked wide!

Something began to hum and whir. It was as if Tim had stirred up a hive of hornets with an ornery stick.

"Oh," gasped Agatha, seeing he had taken the game away, "let *me!*"

She wrenched the key.

Grandma's nostrils *flared!* She might snort up steam, snuff out fire!

"Me!" I cried, and grabbed the key and gave it a huge... *twist!*

The beautiful woman's mouth popped wide.

"Me!"

"Me!"

"Me!"

Grandma suddenly sat up.

We leapt back.

We knew we had, in a way, slapped her alive.

She was born, she was *born!*

Her head swiveled all about. She gaped. She mouthed. And the first thing she said was:

Laughter.

Where one moment we had backed off, now the mad sound drew us near to peer as in a pit where crazy folk are kept with snakes to make them well.

It was a good laugh, full and rich and hearty, and it did not mock, it accepted. It said the world was a wild place, strange, unbelievable, absurd if you wished, but all in all, quite a place. She would not dream to find another. She would not ask to go back to sleep.

She was awake now. We had awakened her. With a glad shout, she would go with it all.

And go she did, out of her sarcophagus, out of her winding sheet, stepping forth, brushing off, looking around as for a mirror. She found it.

The reflections in our eyes.

She was more pleased than disconcerted with what she found there. Her laughter faded to an amused smile.

For Agatha, at the instant of birth, had leapt to hide on the porch.

The Electrical Person pretended not to notice.

She turned slowly on the green lawn near the shady street, gazing all about with new eyes, her nostrils moving as if she breathed the actual air and this the first morn of the lovely Garden and she with no intention of spoiling the game by biting the apple…

Her gaze fixed upon my brother.

"You must be—?"

"Timothy. Tim," he offered.

"And you must be—?"

"Tom," I said.

How clever again of the Fantoccini Company. They knew. She knew. But they had taught her to pretend not to know. That way we could feel great, we were the teachers, telling her what she already knew! How sly, how wise.

"And isn't there another boy?" said the woman.

"Girl!" a disgusted voice cried from somewhere on the porch.

"Whose name is Alicia—?"

"Agatha!" The far voice, started in humiliation, ended in proper anger.

"Algernon, of course."

"Agatha!" Our sister popped up, popped back to hide a flushed face.

"Agatha." The woman touched the word with proper affection. "Well, Agatha, Timothy, Thomas, let me *look* at you."

"No," said I, said Tim, "let us look at *you*. Hey..."

Our voices slid back in our throats.

We drew near her.

We walked in great slow circles round about, skirting the edges of her territory. And her territory extended as far as we could hear the hum of the warm summer hive. For that is exactly what she sounded like. That was her characteristic tune. She made a sound like a season all to herself, a morning early in June when the world wakes to find everything absolutely perfect, fine, delicately attuned, all in balance, nothing disproportioned. Even before you opened your eyes you knew it would be one of those days. Tell the sky what color it must be, and it was indeed. Tell the sun how to crochet its way, pick and choose among leaves to lay out carpetings of bright and dark on the fresh lawn, and pick and lay it did. The bees have been up earliest of all, they have already come and gone, and come and gone again to the meadow fields and returned all golden fuzz on the air, all pollen-decorated, epaulettes at the full, nectar-dripping. Don't you hear them pass? hover? dance their language? telling where all the sweet gums are, the syrups that make bears frolic and lumber in bulked ecstasies, that make boys squirm with unpronounced juices, that make girls leap out of beds to catch from the corners of their eyes their dolphin selves naked aflash on the warm air poised forever in one eternal glass wave.

So it seemed with our electrical friend here on the new lawn in the middle of a special day.

And she a stuff to which we were drawn, lured, spelled, doing our dance, remembering what could not be remembered, needful, aware of her attentions.

Timothy and I, Tom, that is.

Agatha remained on the porch.

But her head flowered above the rail, her eyes followed all that was done and said.

And what was said and done was Tim at last exhaling:

"Hey...your *eyes*..."

Her eyes. Her splendid eyes.

Even more splendid than the lapis lazuli on the sarcophagus lid and on the mask that had covered her bandaged face. These most beautiful eyes in the world looked out upon us calmly, shining.

"Your eyes," gasped Tim, "are the *exact* same color, are like—"

"Like what?"

"My favorite aggies..."

"What could be better than that?" she said.

And the answer was, nothing.

Her eyes slid along on the bright air to brush my ears, my nose, my chin. "And you, Master Tom?"

"Me?"

"How shall we be friends? We must, you know, if we're going to knock elbows about the house the next year..."

"I..." I said, and stopped.

"You," said Grandma, "are a dog mad to bark but with taffy in his teeth. Have you ever given a dog taffy? It's so sad and funny, both. You laugh but hate yourself for laughing. You cry and run to help, and laugh again when his first new bark comes out."

I barked a small laugh remembering a dog, a day, and some taffy.

Grandma turned, and there was my old kite strewn on the lawn. She recognized its problem.

"The string's broken. No. The ball of string's *lost*. You can't fly a kite that way. Here."

She bent. We didn't know what might happen. How could a robot grandma fly a kite for us? She raised up, the kite in her hands.

"Fly," she said, as to a bird.

And the kite flew.

That is to say, with a grand flourish, she let it up on the wind.

And she and the kite were one.

For from the tip of her index finger there sprang a thin bright strand of spider web, all half-invisible gossamer fishline which, fixed to the kite, let it soar a hundred, no, three hundred, no, a thousand feet high on the summer swoons.

Timothy shouted. Agatha, torn between coming and going, let out a cry from the porch. And I, in all my maturity of thirteen years, though I tried not to look impressed, grew taller, taller, and felt a similar cry burst out my lungs, and burst it did. I gabbled and yelled lots of things about how I wished *I* had a finger from which, on a bobbin, I might thread the sky, the clouds, a wild kite all in one.

"If you think *that* is high," said the Electric Creature, "watch *this!*"

With a hiss, a whistle, a hum, the fishline sung out. The kite sank up another thousand feet. And again another thousand, until at last it was a speck of red confetti dancing on the very winds that took jets around the world or changed the weather in the next existence...

"It can't be!" I cried.

"It *is*." She calmly watched her finger unravel its massive stuffs. "I make it as I need it. Liquid inside, like a spider. Hardens when it hits the air, instant thread..."

And when the kite was no more than a specule, a vanishing mote on the peripheral vision of the gods, to quote from older wisemen, why then Grandma, without turning, without looking, without letting her gaze offend by touching, said:

"And, Abigail—?"

"Agatha!" was the sharp response.

O wise woman, to overcome with swift small angers.

"Agatha," said Grandma, not too tenderly, not too lightly, somewhere poised between, "and how shall *we* make do?"

She broke the thread and wrapped it about my fist three times so I was tethered to heaven by the longest, I repeat, longest kite string in the entire history of the world! Wait till I show my friends! I thought. Green! Sour apple green is the color they'll turn!

"Agatha?"

"No way!" said Agatha.

"No way," said an echo.

"There must be some—"

"We'll never be friends!" said Agatha.

"Never be friends," said the echo.

Timothy and I jerked. Where was the echo coming from? Even Agatha, surprised, showed her eyebrows above the porch rail.

Then we looked and saw.

Grandma was cupping her hands like a seashell and from within that shell the echo sounded.

"Never…friends…"

And again faintly dying: "Friends…"

We all bent to hear.

That is we two boys bent to hear.

"No!" cried Agatha.

And ran in the house and slammed the doors.

"Friends," said the echo from the seashell hands. "No."

And far away, on the shore of some inner sea, we heard a small door shut.

And that was the first day.

And there was a second day, of course, and a third and a fourth, with Grandma wheeling in a great circle, and we her planets turning about the central light, with Agatha slowly,

slowly coming in to join, to walk if not run with us, to listen if not hear, to watch if not see, to itch if not touch.

But at least by the end of the first ten days, Agatha no longer fled, but stood in nearby doors, or sat in distant chairs under trees, or if we went out for hikes, followed ten paces behind.

And Grandma? She merely waited. She never tried to urge or force. She went about her cooking and baking apricot pies and left foods carelessly here and there about the house on mousetrap plates for wiggle-nosed girls to sniff and snitch. An hour later, the plates were empty, the buns or cakes gone and without thank you's, there was Agatha sliding down the banister, a mustache of crumbs on her lip.

As for Tim and me, we were always being called up hills by our Electric Grandma, and reaching the top were called down the other side.

And the most peculiar and beautiful and strange and lovely thing was the way she seemed to give complete attention to all of us.

She listened, she really listened to all we said, she knew and remembered every syllable, word, sentence, punctuation, thought, and rambunctious idea. We knew that all our days were stored in her, and that any time we felt we might want to know what we said at X hour at X second on X afternoon, we just named that X and with amiable promptitude, in the form of an aria if we wished, sung with humor, she would deliver forth X incident.

Sometimes we were prompted to test her. In the midst of babbling one day with high fevers about nothing, I stopped. I fixed Grandma with my eye and demanded:

"What did I just say?"

"Oh, er—"

"Come on, spit it out!"

"I think—" she rummaged her purse. "I have it here." From the deeps of her purse she drew forth and handed me:

"Boy! A Chinese fortune cookie!"

"Fresh baked, still warm, open it."

It was almost too hot to touch. I broke the cookie shell and pressed the warm curl of paper out to read:

"—bicycle Champ of the whole West! What did I just say? Come on, spit it out!"

My jaw dropped.

"How did you *do* that?"

"We have our little secrets. The only Chinese fortune cookie that predicts the Immediate Past. Have another?"

I cracked the second shell and read:

"'How did you *do* that?'"

I popped the messages and the piping hot shells into my mouth and chewed as we walked.

"Well?"

"You're a great cook," I said.

And, laughing, we began to run.

And that was another great thing.

She could *keep up.*

Never beat, never win a race, but pump right along in good style, which a boy doesn't mind. A girl ahead of him or beside him is too much to bear. But a girl one or two paces back is a respectful thing, and allowed.

So Grandma and I had some great runs, me in the lead, and both talking a mile a minute.

But now I must tell you the best part of Grandma.

I might not have known at all if Timothy hadn't taken some pictures, and if I hadn't taken some also, and then compared.

When I saw the photographs developed out of our instant Brownies, I sent Agatha, against her wishes, to photograph Grandma a third time, unawares.

Then I took the three sets of pictures off alone, to keep counsel with myself. I never told Timothy and Agatha what I found. I didn't want to spoil it.

But, as I laid the pictures out in my room, here is what I thought and said:

"Grandma, in each picture, looks *different!*"

"Different?" I asked myself.

"Sure. Wait. Just a sec—"

I rearranged the photos.

"Here's one of Grandma near Agatha. And, in it, Grandma looks like...Agatha!

"And in this one, posed with Timothy, she looks like Timothy!

"And this last one, Holy Goll! Jogging along with me, she looks like ugly *me!*"

I sat down, stunned. The pictures fell to the floor.

I hunched over, scrabbling them, rearranging, turning upside down and sidewise. Yes. Holy Goll again, yes!

O that clever Grandmother.

O those Fantoccini people-making people.

Clever beyond clever, human beyond human, warm beyond warm, love beyond love...

And wordless, I rose and went downstairs and found Agatha and Grandma in the same room, doing algebra lessons in an almost peaceful communion. At least there was not outright war. Grandma was still waiting for Agatha to come round. And no one knew what day of what year that would be, or how to make it come faster. Meanwhile—

My entering the room made Grandma turn. I watched her face slowly as it recognized me. And wasn't there the merest ink-wash change of color in those eyes? Didn't the thin film of blood beneath the translucent skin, or whatever liquid they put to pulse and beat in the humanoid forms, didn't it flourish itself suddenly bright in her cheeks and mouth? I am somewhat ruddy. Didn't Grandma suffuse herself more to my color upon my arrival? And her eyes? Watching Agatha-Abigail-Algernon at work, hadn't they been *her* color of blue rather than mine, which are deeper?

More important than that, in the moments as she talked with me, saying, "Good evening," and "How's your homework, my lad?" and such stuff, didn't the bones of her face shift subtly beneath the flesh to assume some fresh racial attitude?

For let's face it, our family is of three sorts. Agatha has the long horse bones of a small English girl who will grow to hunt foxes; Father's equine stare, snort, stomp, and assemblage of skeleton. The skull and teeth are pure English, or as pure as the motley isle's history allows.

Timothy is something else, a touch of Italian from mother's side a generation back. Her family name was Mariano, so Tim has that dark thing firing him, and a small bone structure, and eyes that will one day burn ladies to the ground.

As for me, I am the Slav, and we can only figure this from my paternal grandfather's mother who came from Vienna and brought a set of cheekbones that flared, and temples from which you might dip wine, and a kind of steppeland thrust of nose which sniffed more of Tartar than of Tartan, hiding behind the family name.

So you see it became fascinating for me to watch and try to catch Grandma as she performed her changes, speaking to Agatha and melting her cheekbones to the horse, speaking to Timothy and growing as delicate as a Florentine raven pecking glibly at the air, speaking to me and fusing the hidden plastic stuffs, so I felt Catherine the Great stood there before me.

Now, how the Fantoccini people achieved this rare and subtle transformation I shall never know, nor ask, nor wish to find out. Enough that in each quiet motion, turning here, bending there, affixing her gaze, her secret segments, sections, the abutment of her nose, the sculptured chinbone, the wax-tallow plastic metal forever warmed and was forever susceptible of loving change. Hers was a mask that was all mask but only one face for one person at a time. So in crossing a room, having touched one child, on the way, beneath the skin, the wondrous shift went on, and by the time she reached the next child, why, true mother of *that* child she was! looking upon him or her out of the battlements of their own fine bones.

And when *all* three of us were present and chattering at the same time? Well, then, the changes were miraculously soft, small, and mysterious. Nothing so tremendous as to be caught and noted, save by this older boy, myself, who, watching, became elated and admiring and entranced.

I have never wished to be behind the magician's scenes. Enough that the illusion works. Enough that love is the chemical result. Enough that cheeks are rubbed to happy color, eyes sparked to illumination, arms opened to accept and softly bind and hold...

All of us, that is, except Agatha who refused to the bitter last.

"Agamemnon..."

It had become a jovial game now. Even Agatha didn't mind, but pretended to mind. It gave her a pleasant sense of superiority over a supposedly superior machine.

"Agamemnon!" she snorted, "you *are* a d..."

"Dumb?" said Grandma.

"I wouldn't say that."

"Think it, then, my dear Agonistes Agatha...I am quite flawed, and on names my flaws are revealed. Tom there, is Tim half the time. Timothy is Tobias or Timulty as likely as not..."

Agatha laughed. Which made Grandma make one of her rare mistakes. She put out her hand to give my sister the merest pat. Agatha-Abigail-Alice leapt to her feet.

Agatha-Agamemnon-Alcibiades-Allegra-Alexandra-Allison withdrew swiftly to her room.

"I suspect," said Timothy, later, "because she is beginning to like Grandma."

"Tosh," said I.

"Where do you pick up words like Tosh?"

"Grandma read me some Dickens last night. 'Tosh.' 'Humbug.' 'Balderdash.' 'Blast.' 'Devil take you.' You're pretty smart for your age, Tim."

"Smart, heck. It's obvious, the more Agatha likes Grandma, the more she hates herself for liking her, the more afraid she gets of the whole mess, the more she hates Grandma in the end."

"Can one love someone so much you hate them?"

"Dumb. Of course."

"It *is* sticking your neck out, sure. I guess you hate people when they make you feel naked, I mean sort of on the spot or out in the open. That's the way to play the game, of course. I mean, you don't just love people you must LOVE them with exclamation points."

"You're pretty smart, yourself, for someone so stupid," said Tim.

"Many thanks."

And I went to watch Grandma move slowly back into her battle of wits and stratagems with what's-her-name…

What dinners there were at our house!

Dinners, heck; what lunches, what breakfasts!

Always something new, yet, wisely, it looked or seemed old and familiar. We were never asked, for if you ask children what they want, they do not know, and if you tell what's to be delivered, they reject delivery. All parents know this. It is a quiet war that must be won each day. And Grandma knew how to win without looking triumphant.

"Here's Mystery Breakfast Number Nine," she would say, placing it down. "Perfectly dreadful, not worth bothering with, it made me want to throw up while I was cooking it!"

Even while wondering how a robot could be sick, we could hardly wait to shovel it down.

"Here's Abominable Lunch Number Seventy-seven," she announced. "Made from plastic food bags, parsley, and gum from under theatre seats. Brush your teeth after or you'll taste the poison all afternoon."

We fought each other for more.

Even Abigail-Agamemnon-Agatha drew near and circled round the table at such times, while Father put on the ten pounds he needed and pinkened out his cheeks.

When A. A. Agatha did not come to meals, they were left by her door with a skull and crossbones on a small flag stuck in a baked apple. One minute the tray was abandoned, the next minute gone.

Other times Abigail A. Agatha would bird through during dinner, snatch crumbs from her plate and bird off.

"Agatha!" Father would cry.

"No, wait," Grandma said, quietly. "She'll come, she'll sit. It's a matter of time."

"What's wrong with her?" I asked.

"Yeah, for cri-yi, she's nuts," said Timothy.

"No, she's afraid," said Grandma.

"Of you?" I said, blinking.

"Not of me so much as what I might *do,*" she said.

"You wouldn't do anything to hurt her."

"No, but she thinks I might. We must wait for her to find that her fears have no foundation. If I fail, well, I will send myself to the showers and rust quietly."

There was a titter of laughter. Agatha was hiding in the hall.

Grandma finished serving everyone and then sat at the other side of the table facing Father and pretended to eat. I never found out, I never asked, I never wanted to know, what she did with the food. She was a sorcerer. It simply vanished.

And in the vanishing, Father made comment:

"This food. I've had it before. In a small French restaurant over near Les Deux Magots in Paris, twenty, oh, twenty-five years ago!" His eyes brimmed with tears, suddenly.

"How do you *do* it?" he asked, at last, putting down the cutlery, and looking across the table at this remarkable creature, this device, this what? *woman?*

Grandma took his regard, and ours, and held them simply in her now empty hands, as gifts, and just as gently replied:

"I am given things which I then give to you. I don't *know* that I give, but the giving goes on. You ask what I am? Why, a machine. But even in that answer we know, don't we, more than a machine. I am all the people who thought of me and planned me and built me and set me running. So I am people. I am all the things they wanted to be and perhaps could not be, so they built a great child, a wondrous toy to represent those things."

"Strange," said Father. "When I was growing up, there was a huge out-cry at machines. Machines were bad, evil, they might dehumanize—"

"Some machines do. It's all in the way they are built. It's all in the way they are used. A bear trap is a simple machine that catches and holds and tears. A rifle is a machine that wounds and kills. Well, I am no bear trap. I am no rifle. I am a grandmother machine, which means more than a machine."

"How can you be more than what you seem?"

"No man is as big as his own idea. It follows, then, that any machine that embodies an idea is larger than the man that made it. And what's so wrong with that?"

"I got lost back there about a mile," said Timothy. "Come again?"

"Oh, dear," said Grandma. "How I do hate philosophical discussions and excursions into esthetics. Let me put it this way. Men throw huge shadows on the lawn, don't they? Then, all their lives, they try to run to fit the shadows. But the shadows are always longer. Only at noon can a man fit his own shoes, his own best suit, for a few brief minutes. But now we're in a new age where we can think up a Big Idea and run it around in a machine. That makes the machine more than a machine, doesn't it?"

"So far so good," said Tim. "I guess."

"Well, isn't a motion-picture camera and projector more than a machine? It's a thing that dreams, isn't it? Sometimes fine happy dreams, sometimes nightmares. But to call it a machine and dismiss it is ridiculous."

"I see *that!*" said Tim, and laughed at seeing.

"You must have been invented then," said Father, "by someone who loved machines and hated people who *said* all machines were bad or evil."

"Exactly," said Grandma. "Guido Fantoccini, that was his real name, grew up among machines. And he couldn't stand the clichés anymore."

"Clichés?"

"Those lies, yes, that people tell and pretend they are truths absolute. Man will never fly. That was a cliché truth for a thousand thousand years which turned out to be a lie only a few years ago. The earth is flat, you'll fall off the rim, dragons will dine on you; the great lie told as fact, and Columbus plowed it under. Well, now, how many times have you heard how inhuman machines are, in your life? How many bright fine people have you heard spouting the same tired truths which are in reality lies; all machines destroy, all machines are cold, thoughtless, awful.

"There's a seed of truth there. But only a seed. Guido Fantoccini knew that. And knowing it, like most men of his kind, made him mad. And he could have stayed mad and gone mad forever, but instead did what he had to do; he began to invent machines to give the lie to the ancient lying truth.

"He knew that most machines are amoral, neither bad nor good. But by the way you built and shaped them you in turn shaped men, women, and children to be bad or good. A car, for instance, dead brute, unthinking, an unprogrammed bulk, is the greatest destroyer of souls in history. It makes boy-men greedy for power, destruction, and more destruction. It was never *intended* to do that. But that's how it turned out.

Grandma circled the table, refilling our glasses with clear cold mineral spring water from the tappet in her left forefinger. "Meanwhile, you must use other compensating machines. Machines that throw shadows on the earth that beckon you to run out and fit that wondrous casting-forth. Machines that trim your soul in silhouette like a vast pair of beautiful shears, snipping away the rude brambles, the dire horns and hooves to leave a finer profile. And for that you need examples."

"Examples?" I asked.

"Other people who behave well, and you imitate them. And if you act well enough long enough all the hair drops off and you're no longer a wicked ape."

Grandma sat again.

"So, for thousands of years, you humans have needed kings, priests, philosophers, fine examples to look up to and say, 'They are good, I wish I could be like them. They set the grand good style.' But, being human, the finest priests, the tenderest philosophers make mistakes, fall from grace, and mankind is disillusioned and adopts indifferent skepticism or, worse, motionless cynicism and the good world grinds to a halt while evil moves on with huge strides."

"And you, why, you never make mistakes, you're perfect, you're better than anyone *ever*."

It was a voice from the hall between kitchen and dining room where Agatha, we all knew, stood against the wall listening and now burst forth.

Grandma didn't even turn in the direction of the voice, but went on calmly addressing her remarks to the family at the table.

"Not perfect, no, for what is perfection? But this I do know: being mechanical, I cannot sin, cannot be bribed, cannot be greedy or jealous or mean or small. I do not relish power for power's sake. Speed does not pull me to madness. Sex does not run me rampant through the world. I have time and more than time to collect the information I need around and about an ideal to keep it clean and whole and intact.

Name the value you wish, tell me the Ideal you want and I can see and collect and remember the good that will benefit you all. Tell me how you would like to be: kind, loving, considerate, well-balanced, humane...and let me run ahead on the path to explore those ways to be just that. In the darkness ahead, turn me as a lamp in all directions. I *can* guide your feet."

"So," said Father, putting the napkin to his mouth, "on the days when all of us are busy making lies—"

"I'll tell the truth."

"On the days when we hate—"

"I'll go on giving love, which means attention, which means knowing all about you, all, all, all about you, and you knowing that I know but that most of it I will never tell to anyone, it will stay a warm secret between us, so you will never fear my complete knowledge."

And here Grandma was busy clearing the table, circling, taking the plates, studying each face as she passed, touching Timothy's cheek, my shoulder with her free hand flowing along, her voice a quiet river of certainty bedded in our needful house and lives.

"But," said Father, stopping her, looking her right in the face. He gathered his breath. His face shadowed. At last he let it out. "All this talk of love and attention and stuff. Good God, woman, you, you're not *in* there!"

He gestured to her head, her face, her eyes, the hidden sensory cells behind the eyes, the miniaturized storage vaults and minimal keeps.

"*You're* not *in* there!"

Grandmother waited one, two, three silent beats.

Then she replied: "No. But *you* are. You and Thomas and Timothy and Agatha.

"Everything you ever say, everything you ever do, I'll keep, put away, treasure. I shall be all the things a family forgets it is, but senses, half-remembers. Better than the old family albums you used to leaf through, saying here's this winter, there's that spring, I shall recall what you forget. And though the debate may run another hundred thousand years: What is Love? perhaps we may find that love is the ability of someone to give us back to us. Maybe love is someone seeing and remembering handing us back to ourselves just a trifle better than we had dared to hope or dream…

"I am family memory and, one day perhaps, racial memory, too, but in the round, and at your call. I do not *know* myself. I can neither touch nor taste nor feel on any level. Yet I exist. And my existence means the heightening of your chance to touch and taste and feel. Isn't love in there somewhere in such an exchange? Well…"

She went on around the table, clearing away, sorting and stacking, neither grossly humble nor arthritic with pride.

"What do I know?

"This, above all: the trouble with most families with many children is someone gets lost. There isn't time, it seems, for everyone. Well, I will give equally to all of you. I will share out my knowledge and attention with everyone. I wish to be a great warm pie fresh from the oven, with equal shares to be taken by all. No one will starve. Look! someone cries, and I'll look. Listen! someone cries, and I hear. Run with me on the river path! someone says, and I run. And at dusk I am not tired, nor irritable, so I do not scold out of some tired irritability. My eye stays clear, my voice strong, my hand firm, my attention constant."

"But," said Father, his voice fading, half convinced, but putting up a last faint argument, "you're not *there*. As for love—"

"If paying attention is love, I am love.

"If knowing is love, I am love.

"If helping you not to fall into error and to be good is love, I am love.

"And again, to repeat, there are four of you. Each, in a way never possible before in history, will get my complete attention. No matter if you all speak at once, I can channel and hear this one and that and the other, clearly. No one will go hungry. I will, if you please, and accept the strange word, 'love' you all."

"I *don't* accept!" said Agatha.

And even Grandma turned now to see her standing in the door.

"I won't give you permission, you can't, you mustn't!" said Agatha. "I won't let you! It's lies! You lie. No one loves me. She said she did, but she lied. She *said* but *lied!*"

"Agatha!" cried Father, standing up.

"She?" said Grandma. "Who?"

"Mother!" came the shriek. "Said: Love you! Lies! Love you! Lies! And you're like her! You lie. But you're empty, anyway, and so that's a *double* lie! I hate *her*. Now, I hate *you!*"

Agatha spun about and leapt down the hall.

The front door slammed wide.

Father was in motion, but Grandma touched his arm.

"Let me."

And she walked and then moved swiftly, gliding down the hall and then suddenly, easily, running, yes, running very fast, out the door.

It was a champion sprint by the time we all reached the lawn, the sidewalk, yelling.

Blind, Agatha made the curb, wheeling about, seeing us close, all of us yelling, Grandma way ahead, shouting, too, and Agatha off the curb and out in the street, halfway to the middle, then the middle and suddenly a car, which no one saw, erupting its brakes, its horn shrieking and Agatha flailing about to see and Grandma there with her and hurling her aside and down as the car with fantastic energy and verve selected her from our midst, struck our wonderful electric Guido Fantoccini-produced dream even while she paced upon the air and, hands up to ward off, almost in mild protest, still trying to decide what to say to this bestial machine, over and over she spun and down and away even as the car jolted to a halt and I saw Agatha safe beyond and Grandma, it seemed, still coming down or down and sliding fifty yards away to strike and ricochet and lie strewn and all of us frozen in a line suddenly in the midst of the street with one scream pulled out of all our throats at the same raw instant.

Then silence and just Agatha lying on the asphalt, intact, getting ready to sob.

And still we did not move, frozen on the sill of death, afraid to venture in any direction, afraid to go see what lay beyond the car and Agatha and so we began to wail and, I guess, pray to ourselves as Father stood amongst us: Oh, no, no, we mourned, oh no, God, no, no…

Agatha lifted her already grief-stricken face and it was the face of someone who has predicted dooms and lived to see and now did not want to see or live any more. As we watched, she turned her gaze to the tossed woman's body and tears fell from her eyes. She shut them and covered them and lay back down forever to weep…

I took a step and then another step and then five quick steps and by the time I reached my sister her head was buried deep and her sobs came up out of a place so far down in her I was afraid I could never find her again, she would never come out, no matter how I pried or pleaded or promised or threatened or just plain said. And what little we could hear from Agatha buried there in her own misery, she said over and over again, lamenting, wounded, certain of the old threat known and named and now here forever. "…like I said…told you…lies…lies…liars…all lies…like the other…other…just like…just…just like the other…other…other…"

I was down on my knees holding onto her with both hands, trying to put her back together even though she wasn't broken any way you could see but just feel, because I knew it was no use going on to Grandma, no use at all, so I just touched Agatha and gentled her and wept while Father came up and stood over and knelt down with me and it was like a prayer meeting in the middle of the street and lucky no more cars coming, and I said, choking, "Other what, Ag, other what?"

Agatha exploded two words.

"Other dead!"

"You mean Mom?"

"O Mom," she wailed, shivering, lying down, cuddling up like a baby. "O Mom, dead, O Mom and now Grandma dead, she promised always, always, to love, to love, promised to be different, promised, promised and now look, look... I hate her, I hate Mom, I hate her, I hate *them!*"

"Of course," said a voice. "It's only natural. How foolish of me not to have known, not to have seen."

And the voice was so familiar we were all stricken.

We all jerked.

Agatha squinched her eyes, flicked them wide, blinked, and jerked half up, staring.

"How silly of me," said Grandma, standing there at the edge of our circle, our prayer, our wake.

"Grandma!" we all said.

And she stood there, taller by far than any of us in this moment of kneeling and holding and crying out. We could only stare up at her in disbelief.

"You're dead!" cried Agatha. "The car—"

"Hit me," said Grandma, quietly. "Yes. And threw me in the air and tumbled me over and for a few moments there was a severe concussion of circuitries. I might have feared a disconnection, if fear is the word. But then I sat up and gave myself a shake and the few molecules of paint, jarred loose on one printed path or another, magnetized back in position and resilient creature that I am, unbreakable thing that I am, *here* I am."

"I thought you were—" said Agatha.

"And only natural," said Grandma. "I mean, anyone else, hit like that, tossed like that. But, O my dear Agatha, not me. And now I see why you were afraid and never trusted me. You didn't know. And I had not as yet proved my singular ability to survive. How dumb of me not to have thought to show you. Just a second." Somewhere in her head, her body, her being, she fitted together some invisible tapes, some old information made new by interblending. She nodded. "Yes. There. A book of child-raising, laughed at by some few people years back when the woman who wrote the book said, as final advice to parents: 'Whatever you do, don't die. Your children will never forgive you.'"

"Forgive," some one of us whispered.

"For how can children understand when you just up and go away and never come back again with no excuse, no apologies, no sorry note, nothing."

"They can't," I said.

"So," said Grandma, kneeling down with us beside Agatha who sat up now, new tears brimming her eyes, but a different kind of tears, not tears that drowned, but tears that washed clean. "So your mother ran away to death. And after that, how *could* you trust anyone? If everyone left vanished finally, who was there to trust? So when I came, half wise, half ignorant, I should have known, I did not know, why you would not accept me. For, very simply and honestly, you feared I might not stay, that I lied, that I was vulnerable, too. And two leavetakings, two deaths, were one too many in a single year. But now, do you *see*, Abigail?"

"Agatha," said Agatha, without knowing she corrected.

"Do you understand, I shall always, always be here?"

"Oh, yes," cried Agatha, and broke down into a solid weeping in which we all joined, huddled together and cars drew up and stopped to see just how many people were hurt and how many people were getting well right there.

. . .

End of story.

. . .

Well, not quite the end.

We lived happily ever after.

Or rather we lived together, Grandma, Agatha-Agamemnon-Abigail, Timothy, and I, Tom, and Father, and Grandma calling us to frolic in great fountains of Latin and Spanish and French, in great seaborne gouts of poetry like Moby Dick sprinkling the deeps with his Versailles jet somehow lost in calms and found in storms; Grandma a constant, a clock, a pendulum, a face to tell all time by at noon, or in the middle of sick nights when, raved with fever, we saw her forever by our beds, never gone, never away, always waiting, always speaking kind words, her cool hand icing our hot brows, the tappet of her uplifted forefinger unsprung to let a twine of cold mountain water touch our flannel tongues. Ten thousand dawns she cut our wildflower lawn, ten thousand nights she wandered, remembering the dust molecules that fell in the still hours before dawn, or sat whispering some lesson she felt needed teaching to our ears while we slept snug.

Until at last, one by one, it was time for us to go away to school, and when at last the youngest, Agatha, was all packed, why Grandma packed, too.

On the last day of summer that last year, we found Grandma down in the front room with various packets and suitcases, knitting, waiting, and though she had often spoken of it, now that the time came we were shocked and surprised.

"Grandma!" we all said. "What are you doing?"

"Why going off to college, in a way, just like you," she said. "Back to Guido Fantoccini's, to the Family."

"The Family?"

"Of Pinocchios, that's what he called us for a joke, at first. The Pinocchios and himself Gepetto. And then later gave us his own name: the Fantoccini. Anyway, you have been my family here. Now I go back to my even larger family there, my brothers, sisters, aunts, cousins, all robots who—"

"Who do *what?*" asked Agatha.

"It all depends," said Grandma. "Some stay, some linger. Others go to be drawn and quartered, you might say, their parts distributed to other machines who have need of repairs. They'll weigh and find me wanting or not wanting. It may be I'll be just the one they need tomorrow and off I'll go to raise another batch of children and beat another batch of fudge."

"Oh, they mustn't draw and quarter you!" cried Agatha.

"No!" I cried, with Timothy.

"My allowance," said Agatha, "I'll pay anything…"

Grandma stopped rocking and looked at the needles and the pattern of bright yarn. "Well, I wouldn't have said, but now you ask and I'll tell. For a very *small* fee, there's a room, the room of the Family, a large dim parlor, all quiet and nicely decorated, where as many as thirty or forty of the Electric Women sit and rock and talk, each in her turn. I have not been there. I am, after all, freshly born, comparatively new. For a small fee, very small, each month and year, that's where I'll be, with all the others like me, listening to what they've learned of the world and, in my turn, telling how it was with Tom and Tim and Agatha and how fine and happy we were. And I'll tell all I learned from you."

"But…you taught *us!*"

"Do you *really* think that?" she said. "No, it was turnabout, roundabout, learning both ways. And it's all in here, everything you flew into tears about or laughed over, why, I have it all. And I'll tell it to the others just as they tell their boys and girls and life to me. We'll sit there, growing wiser and calmer and better every year and every year, ten, twenty, thirty years. The Family knowledge will double, quadruple, the wisdom will not be lost. And we'll be waiting there in that sitting room, should you ever need us for your own children in time of illness, or, God prevent, deprivation or death. There we'll be, growing old but not old, getting closer to the time, perhaps, someday, when we live up to our first strange joking name."

"The Pinocchios?" asked Tim.

Grandma nodded.

I knew what she meant. The day when, as in the old tale, Pinocchio had grown so worthy and so fine that the gift of life had been given him. So I saw them, in future years, the entire family of Fantoccini, the Pinocchios, trading and re-trading, murmuring and whispering their knowledge in the great parlors of philosophy, waiting for the day. The day that could never come.

Grandma must have read that thought in our eyes.

"We'll see," she said. "Let's just wait and see."

"Oh, Grandma," cried Agatha and she was weeping as she had wept many years before. "You don't have to wait. You're alive. You've always been alive to us!"

And she caught hold of the old woman and we all caught hold for a long moment and then ran off up in the sky to faraway schools and years and her last words to us before we let the helicopter swarm us away into autumn were these:

"When you are very old and gone childish-small again, with childish ways and childish yens and, in need of feeding, make a wish for the old teacher nurse, the dumb yet wise companion, send for me. I will come back. We shall inhabit the nursery again, never fear."

"Oh, we shall never be old!" we cried. "That will never happen!"

"Never! Never!"

And we were gone.

And the years are flown.

And we are old now, Tim and Agatha and I.

Our children are grown and gone, our wives and husbands vanished from the earth and now, by Dickensian coincidence, accept it as you will or not accept, back in the old house, we three.

I lie here in the bedroom which was my childish place seventy, O seventy, believe it, seventy years ago. Beneath this wallpaper is another layer and yet another-times-three to the old wallpaper covered over when I was nine. The wallpaper is peeling. I see peeking from beneath, old elephants, familiar tigers, fine and amiable zebras, irascible crocodiles. I have sent for the paperers to carefully remove all but that last layer. The old animals will live again on the walls, revealed.

And we have sent for someone else.

The three of us have called:

Grandma! You said you'd come back when we had need.

We are surprised by age, by time. We are old. We *need*.

And in three rooms of a summer house very late in time, three old children rise up, crying out in their heads: We *loved* you! We *love* you!

There! There! in the sky, we think, waking at morn. Is that the delivery machine? Does it settle to the lawn?

There! There on the grass by the front porch. Does the mummy case arrive?

Are our names inked on ribbons wrapped about the lovely form beneath the golden mask?!

And the kept gold key, forever hung on Agatha's breast, warmed and waiting? Oh God, will it, after all these years, will it wind, will it set in motion, will it, dearly, *fit?!*

MARIONETTES INC.

They walked slowly down the street at about ten in the evening, talking quietly, both about thirty-five, both eminently sober.

"But why so early?" said Smith.

"Because," said Braling.

"Your first night out in years and you go home at ten o'clock."

"Nerves, I suppose."

"What I wonder is how you ever managed it? I've been trying to get you out for ten years for a quiet drink. And now, on the one night, you insist on turning in early."

"Mustn't crowd my luck," said Braling.

"What did you do, put sleeping powder in your wife's coffee?"

"That would be unethical, no. You'll see soon enough."

They turned a corner. "Honestly, Braling, I hate to say this, but you *have* been patient with her. You may not admit it to me, but marriage has been awful for you; hasn't it?"

"I wouldn't say that."

"It's got around, anyway, here and there, how she got you to marry her. That time back in 1979 when you were going to Rio—"

"Dear Rio, I never *did* see it after all my plans."

"And how she tore her clothes and rumpled her hair and threatened to call the police unless you married her."

"She always was nervous, Smith, understand."

"It was more than unfair. You didn't love her. You told her as much, didn't you?"

"I recall that I was quite firm on the subject."

"But you married her anyhow."

"I had my business to think of, as well as my mother and father. A thing like that would have killed them."

"And it's been ten years."

"Yes," said Braling, his gray eyes steady. "But I think perhaps it might change now. I think what I've waited for has come about. Look here."

MARIONETTES, INC.

He drew forth a long blue ticket.

"Why, it's a ticket for Rio on the Thursday rocket!"

"Yes, I'm finally going to make it."

"But how wonderful, you *do* deserve it! But won't *she* object? Cause trouble?"

• • •

Braling smiled nervously. "She won't know I'm gone. I'll be back in a month and no one the wiser, except you."

Smith sighed. "I wish I were going with."

"Poor Smith, *your* marriage hasn't exactly been roses, has it?"

"Not exactly, married to a woman who overdoes it. I mean, after all, when you've been married ten years, you don't expect a woman to sit on your lap for two hours every evening, call you at work twelve times a day and talk baby-talk. And it seems to me that in the last month she's gotten worse. I wonder if perhaps she isn't just a little simpleminded?"

"Ah, Smith, always the conservative. Well, here's my house. Now, would you like to know my secret? How did I make it out this evening?"

"Will you really tell?"

"Look up, there!" said Braling.

They both stared up through the dark air.

In the window above them, on the second floor, a shade was raised. A man about thirty-five years old, with a touch of gray at either temple, sad gray eyes, and a small thin moustache looked down at them.

"Why, that's *you!*" cried Smith:

"Sh-h-h, not so loud!" Braling waved upward. The man in the window gestured significantly and vanished.

"I must be insane," said Smith.

"Hold on a moment."

They waited.

The street door of the apartment opened and the tall spare gentleman with the moustache and the grieved eyes came out to meet them.

"Hello, Braling," he said.

"Hello, Braling," said Braling.

They were identical.

Smith stared. "Is this your twin brother? I never knew—"

"No, no," said Braling, quietly. "Bend close. Put your ear to Braling Two's chest."

Smith hesitated and then leaned forward to place his head against the uncomplaining ribs.

Tic-tic-tic-tic-tic-tic-tic-tic.

"Oh no ! It *can't* be!"

MARIONETTES, INC.

"It is."

"Let me listen again."

Tic-tic-tic-tic-tic-tic-tic-tic.

Smith staggered back and fluttered his eyelids, appalled. He reached out and touched the warm hands and the cheeks of the thing.

"Where'd you get him?"

"Isn't he excellently fashioned?"

"Incredible. Where?"

"Give the man your cards Braling Two."

Braling Two did a magic trick and produced a white card:

MARIONETTES, INC.

Duplicate self or friends; new humanoid-plastic 1990 models, guaranteed against all physical wear. From $7,600 to our $15,000 deluxe model.

"No," said Smith.

"Yes," said Braling.

"Naturally," said Braling Two.

"How long has this gone on?"

"I've had him for a month. I keep him in the cellar in a tool box. My wife never goes downstairs, and I have the only lock and key to that box. Tonight, I said I wished to take a walk to buy a cigar. I went down to the cellar and took Braling Two out of his box and sent him back up to sit with my wife while I came on out to see you, Smith."

"Wonderful! He even *smells* like you; Bond Street and melachrinos."

"It may be splitting hairs, but I think it highly ethical. After all, what my wife wants most of all is *me*. This Marionette *is* me to the hairiest detail, I've been home all evening. I shall be home with her for the next month. In the meantime another gentleman will be in Rio after ten years of waiting. When I return from Rio, Braling Two here will go back in his box."

. . .

Smith thought that over for a minute or two. "Will he walk around without sustenance for a month?" he finally asked.

"For six months if necessary, and he's built to do everything, eat, sleep, perspire, everything, natural as natural is. You'll take good care of my wife, won't you, Braling Two?"

"Your wife is rather nice," said Braling Two. "I've grown rather fond of her."

Smith was beginning to tremble. "How long has Marionettes, Inc. been in business?"

"Secretly, for two years."

"Could I—I mean, is there a possibility—" Smith took his friend's elbow earnestly. "Can you tell me where I can get one, a robot, a marionette, for myself? You will give me the address, won't you?"

"Here you are."

Smith took the card and turned it round and round. "Thank you," he said. "You don't know what this means. Just a little respite. A night or so, once a month even. My wife loves me so much she can't bear to have me gone an hour. I love her dearly, you know, but remember the old Oscar Wilde poem: 'Love will fly if held too lightly, love will die if held too tightly.' I just want her to relax her grip a little bit."

"You're lucky, at least, that your wife loves you; Hate's my problem. Not so easy."

"Oh, Nettie loves me madly. It will be my task to make her love me comfortably."

"Good luck to you, Smith. Do drop around while I'm in Rio. It will seem strange, if you suddenly stop calling by, to my wife. You're to treat Braling Two, here, just like me."

"Right! Good-by. And thank you."

Smith went smiling down the street. Braling and Braling Two turned and walked into the apartment hall.

On the cross-town bus, Smith whistled softly, turning the white card in his fingers:

Clients must be pledged to secrecy, for while an act is pending in Congress to legalize MARIONETTES, INC., it is still a felony, if caught, to use one.

"Well," said Smith.

Clients must have a mould made of their body and a color index check of their eyes, lips, hair, skin, etc. Clients must expect to wait for two months until their model is finished.

"Not so long," thought Smith. "Two months from now my ribs will have a chance to mend from the crushing they've taken. Two months from now my hand will heal from being so constantly held. Two months from now my bruised under-lip will begin to reshape itself. I don't mean to sound *ungrateful.*" He flipped the card over:

MARIONETTES, INC. is two years old and has a fine record of satisfied customers behind it. Our motto is "No Strings Attached." Address: 43 South Wesley Drives

The bus pulled to his stop, he alighted, and while humming up the stairs he thought, Nettie and I have fifteen thousand in our joint bank account. I'll just slip eight thousand out as a business venture, you might say. The Marionette will probably pay back my money, with interest, in many ways. Nettie needn't know. He unlocked the door and in a minute was in the bedroom. There lay Nettie, pale, huge, and piously asleep.

"Dear Nettie." He was almost overwhelmed with remorse at her innocent face there in the semi-darkness. "If you were awake you would smother me with kisses and coo in my ear. Really, you make me feel like a criminal. You have been such a good, loving wife. Some times it is impossible for me to believe you married me instead of that Bud Chapman you once liked. It seems that in the last month you have loved me more wildly than *ever* before."

Tears came to his eyes. Suddenly he wished to kiss her, confess his love, tear up the card, forget the whole business. But as he moved to do this, his hand ached and his ribs cracked and groaned. He stopped, with a pained look in his eyes, and turned away. He moved out into the hall and through the dark rooms. Humming, he opened the kidney-desk in the library and filched out the bank book. "Just take eight thousand dollars is all," he said. "No more than that." He stopped. "Wait a minute."

• • •

He rechecked the bank book frantically. "Hold on here!" he cried. "Ten thousand dollars is missing!" He leaped up. "There's only five thousand left? What's she done? What's Nettie done with it? More hats, more clothes, more perfume! Or wait—I know! She bought that little house on the Hudson she's been talking about for months, without so much as a by your leave!"

He stormed into the bedroom, righteous and indignant. What did she mean, taking their money like this? He bent over her. "Nettie!" he shouted. "Nettie, wake up!"

She did not stir. "What've you done with my money!" he bellowed.

She stirred fitfully. The light from the street flushed over her beautiful cheeks.

There was something about her. His heart throbbed violently. His tongue dried. He shivered. His knees suddenly turned to water. He collapsed. "Nettie, Nettie!" he cried. "What've you done with my money!"

And then, the horrid thought. And then the terror and the loneliness engulfed him. And then the fever and disillusionment. For, without desiring to do so, he bent forward and yet forward again until his fevered ear was resting firmly and irrevocably upon her sound pink bosom. "Nettie!" he cried.

Tic-tic-tic-tic-tic-tic-tic-tic-tic-tic.

MARIONETTES, INC.

• • •

As Smith walked away down the avenue in the night, Braling and Braling Two turned in at the door to the apartment. "I'm glad he'll be happy, too," said Braling.

"Yes," said Braling Two, abstractedly.

"Well, it's the cellar box for you, B-Two." Braling guided the other creature's elbow down the stairs to the cellar.

"That's what I want to talk to you about," said Braling Two, as they reached the concrete floor and walked across it. "The cellar. I don't like it: I don't like that tool box."

"I'll try and fix up something more comfortable."

"Marionettes are made to move not lie still. How would you like to lie in a box most of the time?"

"Well—"

"You wouldn't like it at all. I keep running. There's no way to shut me off. I'm perfectly alive and I have feelings."

"It'll only be a few days now, I'll be off to Rio and you won't have to stay in the box. You can live upstairs."

Braling Two gestured irritably. "And when you come back from having a good time, back in the box I go."

Braling said, "They didn't tell me at the Marionette Shop that I'd get a difficult specimen."

"There's a lot they don't know about us," said Braling Two. "We're pretty new. And we're sensitive. I hate the idea of you going off and laughing and lying in the sun in Rio while we're stuck here in the cold."

"But I've wanted that trip all my life," sand Braling quietly.

He squinted his eyes and could see the sea and the mountains and the yellow sand and the sound of the waves was good to his inward mind. The sun was fine on his bared shoulders. The wine was most excellent.

"*I'll* never get to go to Rio," said the other man. "Have you thought of that?"

"No, I—"

"And another thing. Your wife."

"What about her?" asked Braling, beginning to edge toward the door.

"I've grown quite fond of her."

"I'm glad you're enjoying your employment." Braling licked his lips nervously.

"I'm afraid you don't understand. I think—I'm in love with her."

• • •

Braling took another step and froze. "You're *what?*"

"And I've been thinking," said Braling Two. "How nice it is in Rio and how I'll never get there and I've thought about your wife and—I think we could be very happy."

MARIONETTES, INC.

"T-that's nice." Braling strolled as casually as he could to the cellar door. "You won't mind waiting a moment, will you, I have to make a phone call."

"To whom?" Braling Two frowned.

"No one important."

"To Marionettes Incorporated? To tell them to come get me?"

"No, no, nothing like that!" He tried to rush out the door.

A metal-firm grip seized his wrists. "Don't run!"

"Take your hands off! Did my wife put you up to this?"

"No."

"Did she guess? Did she talk to you? Does she know? Is *that* it?" He screamed. A hand clapped over his mouth.

"You'll never know, will you." Braling Two smiled delicately. "You'll never know."

Braling struggled. "She *must* have guessed, she *must* have affected you!"

Braling Two said, "I'm going to put you in the box, lock it, and lose the key. Then I'll buy another Rio ticket for your wife."

"Now, now, wait a minute, hold on, don't be rash, let's talk this over!"

"Good-by, Braling."

Braling stiffened. "What do you mean, good-by!"

Ten minutes later, Mrs. Braling awoke. She put her hand to her cheek. Someone had just kissed it. She shivered and looked up. "Why—you haven't done that in years," she murmured.

"We'll see what we can do about that," someone said.

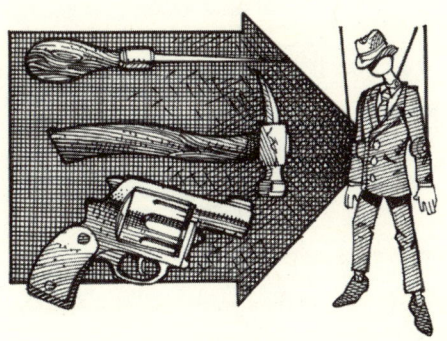

CHANGELING

By eight o'clock she had placed the long cigarettes and the wine crystals and the silver bucket of thin shaved ice packed around the green bottle. She stood looking at the room, each picture neat, ashtrays conveniently disposed. She plumped a lounge pillow and stepped back, her eyes squinting. Then she hurried into the bathroom and returned with the strychnine bottle, which she laid under a magazine on an end-table. She had already hidden a hammer and an icepick.

She was ready.

Seeming to know this, the phone rang. When she answered, a voice said:

"I'm coming up."

He was in the elevator now, floating silently up the iron throat of the house, fingering his accurate little moustache, adjusting his white summer evening coat and black tie. He would be smoothing his gray-blonde hair, that handsome man of fifty still able to visit handsome women of thirty-three, fresh, convivial, ready for the wine and the rest of it.

"You're a faker!" she whispered to the closed door a moment before he rapped.

"Good evening, Martha," he said. "Are you just going to stand there, looking?" She kissed him quietly. "Was that a kiss?" he wondered, his blue eyes warmly amused. "Here." He gave her a better one.

Her eyes closed, she thought, is this different from last week, last month, last year? What makes me suspicious? Some little thing. Something she couldn't even tell, it was so minor. He had changed subtly and drastically. So drastically in fact, so completely that she had begun to stay awake nights two months ago. She had taken to riding the helicopters at three in the morning out to the beach and back to see all-night films projected on the clouds near The Point, films that had been made way back in 1955, huge memories in the ocean mist over the dark waters, with the voices drifting in like gods' voices with the tide. She was constantly tired.

"Not much response." He held her away and surveyed her critically. "Is anything wrong, Martha?"

"Nothing," she said. Everything, she thought. You, she thought. Where are you tonight, Leonard? Who are you dancing with far away, or drinking with in an apartment, on the other side of town, who are you being lovably polite with? For you most certainly are not here in this room, and I intend to prove it.

"What's this?" he said, looking down. "A hammer? Have you been hanging pictures, Martha?"

"No, I'm going to hit you with it," she said, and laughed.

"Of course," he said, smiling. "Well, perhaps this will make you change your mind." He drew forth a plush case, inside which was a pearl necklace.

"Oh, Leonard!" She put it on with trembling fingers and turned to him, excited. "You are good to me."

"It's nothing at all," he said.

At these times, she almost forgot her suspicions. She had everything with him, didn't she? There was no sign of his losing interest, was there? Certainly not. He was just as kind and gentle and generous. He never came without something for her wrist or her finger. Why did she feel so lonely with him then? Why didn't she feel with him? Perhaps it had started with that picture in the paper two months ago. A picture of him and Alice Summers in The Club on the night of April 17th. She hadn't seen the picture until a month later and then she had spoken of it to him:

"Leonard, you didn't tell me you took Alice Summers to The Club on the night of April seventeenth."

"Didn't I, Martha? Well, I did."

"But wasn't that one of the nights you were here with me?"

"I don't see how it could have been. We have supper and play symphonies and drink wine until early morning."

"I'm sure you were here with me April seventeenth, Leonard."

"You're a little drunk, my dear. Do you keep a diary?"

"I'm not a child."

"There you are then. No diary, no record. I was here the night before or the night after. Come on now, Martha, drink up."

But that hadn't settled it. She had not gone to sleep that night with thinking and being positive he had been with her on April 17th. It was impossible, of course. He couldn't be in two places.

They both stood looking down at the hammer on the floor. She picked it up and put it on a table. "Kiss me," she said, quite suddenly, for she wanted now, more than ever, to be certain of this thing.

He evaded her and said, "First, the wine."

"No," she insisted, and kissed him.

There it was. The difference. The little change. There was no way to tell anyone, or even describe it. It would be like trying to describe a rainbow to a blind man. But there was a subtle chemical difference to his kiss. It was no longer the kiss of Mr. Leonard Hill. It approximated the kiss of Leonard Hill but was sufficiently different to set a subconscious wheel rolling in her. What would an analysis of the faint moisture on his lips reveal? Some bacterial lack? And as for the lips themselves, were or were they not harder, or softer, than before? Some small difference.

"All right, now the wine," she said, and opened it. She poured his glass full. "Oh, will you get some mats from the kitchen to set them on?" While he was gone she poured the strychnine in his glass. He returned with the mats to set the glasses on and picked up his drink.

"To us," he said.

• • •

Good Lord, she thought, what if I'm wrong? What if this is really him? What if I'm just some wild paranoid sort of creature, really insane and not aware of it?

"To us." She raised her glass.

He drained his at a gulp, as always. "My God," he said, wincing. "That's horrible stuff. Where did you get it?"

"At Modesti's."

"Well, don't get any more. Here, I'd better ring for more."

"Never mind, I have more in the refrigerator."

When she brought the new bottle in, he was sitting there, clever and alive and fresh. "You look wonderful," she said.

"Feel fine. You're beautiful. I think I love you more tonight than ever."

She waited for him to fall sidewise and stare the stare of the dead. "Here we go," he said, opening the second bottle.

When the second bottle was empty, an hour had passed. He was telling witty little stories and holding her hand and kissing her gently now and again. At last he turned to her and said, "You seem quiet tonight. Martha? Anything wrong?"

"No," she said.

She had seen the news item last week, the item that had finally set her worrying and planning, that had explained her loneliness in his presence. About the marionettes. Marionettes, Incorporated. Not that they really existed, surely not. But there was a rumor. Police were investigating.

Life-size marionettes, mechanical, stringless, secretive, duplicates of real people. One might buy them for ten thousand dollars on some distant black market. One could be measured for a replica of one's self. If one grew weary of social functions, one could send the replica out to wine, to dine, to shake hands, to trade gossip with Mrs. Rinehart on your left, Mr. Simmons on your right, Miss Glenner across the table.

Think of the political tirades one might miss! Think of the bad shows one need never see. Think of the dull people one could snub without actually snubbing. And, last of all, think of the jeweled loved ones you could ignore, yet not ignore. What would a good slogan be? She Need Never Know? Don't Tell Your Best Friends? It Walks, It Talks, It Sneezes, It Says "Mama"?

When she thought of this she became almost hysterical. Of course it had not been proven that such things as Marionettes existed. Just a sly rumor, with enough to it to make a sensitive person crawl with horror.

"Abstracted again," he said, interrupting her quietness. "There you go, wandering off. What's in that pretty head of yours?"

She looked at him. It was foolish; at any moment he might convulse and die. Then she would be sorry for her jealousy.

Without thinking, she said, "Your mouth; it tastes funny."

"Dear me," he said. "I shall have to see to that, eh?"

"It's tasted funny for some time."

For the first time he seemed concerned. "Has it? I'm sorry. I'll see my doctor."

"It's not that important." She felt her heart beating quickly and she was cold. It was his mouth. After all, no matter how perfect chemists were; could they analyze and reproduce the exact taste? Hardly. Taste was individual. Taste was one thing to her, something else to another. There was where they had fallen down. She would not put up with it another minute. She walked over to the other couch, reached down and drew out the gun.

"What's that?" he said, looking at it. "Oh my God," he laughed. "A gun. How dramatic."

"I've caught on to you," she said.

"Is there anything to catch on to?" he wanted to know, calmly, his mouth straight, his eyes twinkling.

"You've been lying to me. You haven't been here in eight weeks or more," she said.

"Is that true? Where have I been, then?"

"With Alice Summers, I wouldn't doubt. I'll bet you're with her right now."

"Is that possible?" he asked.

"I don't know Alice Summers, I've never met her, but I think I'll call her apartment right now."

"Do that," he said, looking straight at her.

"I will," she said, moving to the phone. Her hand shook so that she could hardly dial information. While waiting for the number to come through she watched Leonard and he watched her with the eye of a psychiatrist witnessing a not-unusual phenomenon.

"You are badly off," he said. "My dear Martha—"

"Sit down!"

"My dear Martha," he moved back in the couch, chuckling softly. "What have you been reading?"

"About the Marionettes is all."

"That poppycock? Good God, Martha, I'm ashamed of you. It's not true. I looked into it!"

"What!"

"Of course!" he cried, in delight. "I have so many social obligations, and then my first wife came back from India as you know and demanded my time and I thought how fine it would be if I had a replica of myself made, as bait you might say, to turn my wife off my trail, to keep her busy, how nice, eh? But it was all false. Just one of those Sunday supplement fantasies, I assure you. Now put that phone down and come have another glass of wine."

She had stood staring at him in bewilderment during all of his pronouncement. She had almost dropped the phone, believing him, until he said the word 'wine'. Then she shook herself and said, "Wait a minute. You can't talk me out of this! I gave you some poison a while ago, enough to kill six men. You haven't showed a sign of it. That proves something, doesn't it?"

"It proves nothing at all. It merely proves that your chemist gave you the wrong bottle, is probably more like it. I'm sorry to disappoint you, but I feel fine. Put down that phone now, Martha, and be sensible."

She held the phone in her hand. A voice said, "That number is A B one two two fower niyen."

"I just want to be certain," she said.

"All right," he shrugged. "But if I'm not to be trusted I'm afraid I won't come back to see you again. What you need, my dear lady, is a psychiatrist, in the worst way. You're right on the edge!"

"Hello, operator? Give me A B one two two four nine."

"Martha, don't." he said, sitting there, one hand out.

The phone rang and rang at the other end. Finally a voice answered. Martha listened to it for a minute and then put the phone down.

• • •

Leonard looked into her face and said, "There. Are you satisfied?"

"Yes," she said. Her mouth was thick. She raised the gun.

"Don't!" he screamed. He stood up.

"That was your voice on the other end," she said. "You were with her!"

"You're insane!" he cried. "Oh, God, Martha, don't, it's a mistake, that was someone else, you're so overwrought you thought it sounded like me!"

She fired the gun once, twice, three times.

He fell to the floor.

She came to stand over him. She was afraid, and she began to cry. The fact that he had actually fallen at her feet had surprised her. She had imagined that a Marionette would only stand there and laugh at her, alive, immortal.

I was wrong, she thought. I am insane. This is Leonard Hill and I've killed him.

He lay with his eyes closed, his mouth moving. "Martha," he said. "Why didn't you leave well enough alone. Oh, Martha."

"I'll call a doctor," she said.

"No, no, no." And suddenly he began to laugh. "You've got to know sometime. And now that you've done this, oh you fool, I may as well admit it."

The gun fell from her fingers.

"I," he said, choking on laughter. "I haven't been here with you for a—for a year!"

"What?"

"A year, twelve months! Yes, Martha, twelve months!"

"You're lying!"

"Oh, you won't believe me now, will you? What's changed you in ten seconds? Do you think I'm Leonard Hill? Forget it!"

"Then that was you? At Alice Summers' apartment just now?"

"Me? No! I started with Alice a year ago, when first I left you!"

"Left me?"

"Yes, left, left, left!" he shouted, and laughed, lying there.

"I'm an old man, Martha, old and tired. The rat-race was too much for me. I thought I needed a change. So I went on to Alice and tired of her. And went on to Helen Kingsley, you remember her, don't you? And tired of her. And on to Ann Montgomery. And that didn't last. Oh, Martha, there are at least six duplicates of me, mechanical hypocrites, ticking away tonight, in all parts of the town, keeping six people happy. And do you know what I am doing, the real I?

"I'm home in bed early for the first time in thirty years, reading my little book of Montaigne's essays and enjoying it and drinking a hot glass of chocolate milk and turning out the lights at ten o'clock. I've been asleep for an hour now, and I shall sleep the sleep of the innocent until morning and arise refreshed and free."

"Stop!" she shrieked.

"I've got to tell you," he said. "You've cut several of my ligaments with your bullets. I can't get up. The doctors, if they came, would find me out anyway, I'm not that perfect. Perfect enough, but not that good. Oh, Martha, I didn't want to hurt you. Believe me. I wanted only your happiness. That's why I was so careful with my planned withdrawal, I spent fifteen thousand dollars for this replica, perfect in every detail. There are variables. The saliva for one. A regrettable error. It set you off. But you must know that I loved you."

She would fall at any moment, writhing into insanity, she thought. He had to be stopped from talking.

"And when I saw how the others loved me," he whispered to the ceiling, eyes wide, "I had to provide replicas for them, poor dears. They love me so. You won't tell them, will you, Martha? Promise me you won't give the show away. I'm a very tired old man, and I want only peace, a book, some milk and a lot of sleep. You won't call them up and give it away?"

"All this year, this whole year, I've been alone, alone every night," she said, the coldness filling her. "Talking to a mechanical horror! In love with nothingness! Alone all that time, when I could have been out with someone real!"

"I can still love you, Martha."

"Oh God!" she cried, and seized up the hammer.

"Don't, Martha!"

She smashed his head in and beat at his chest and his thrashing arms and wild legs. She beat at the soft head until steel shone through, and sudden explosions of wire and brass coggery showered about the room with metal tinkles.

"I love you," said the man's mouth. She struck it with the hammer and the tongue fell out. The glass eyes rolled on the carpet. She pounded at the thing until it was strewn like the remains of a child's electric train on the floor. She laughed while she was doing it.

In the kitchen she found several cardboard boxes. She loaded the cogs and wires and metal into these and sealed the tops. Ten minutes later she had summoned the house-boy from below.

"Deliver these packages to Mr. Leonard Hill, 17 Elm Drive," she said, and tipped the boy. "Right now, tonight. Wake him up, tell him it's a surprise package from Martha."

"A surprise package from Martha," said the boy,

After the door closed, she sat on the couch with the gun in her hand, turning it over and over, listening. The last thing she heard in her life was the sound of the packages being carried down the hall, the metal jingling softly, cog against cog, wire against wire, fading.

PUNISHMENT WITHOUT CRIME

The sign on the door said: MARIONETTES, INC.

"You wish to kill your wife?" said the dark man at the desk.

"Yes. No…not exactly. I mean…"

"Name?"

"Hers or mine?"

"Yours."

"George Hill."

"Address?"

"11 South St. James, Glenview."

The man wrote this down, emotionlessly. "Your wife's name?"

"Katherine."

"Age?"

"Thirty-one."

Then came a swift series of questions. Color of hair, eyes, skin, favorite perfume, texture and size index. "Have you a dimensional photo of her? And her lipstick…?"

An hour later, George Hill was perspiring.

"That's all." The dark man arose and scowled. "You still want to go through with it."

"Yes."

"Sign here."

He signed.

"You know this is illegal?"

"Yes."

"And that we're in no way responsible for what happens to you as a result of your request?"

"For God's sake!" cried George. "You've kept me long enough. Let's get on!"

The man smiled faintly. "It'll take three hours to prepare the marionette of your wife. Sleep awhile, it'll help your nerves. The third mirror room on your left is unoccupied."

George moved in a slow numbness to the mirror room. He lay on the blue velvet cot, his body pressure causing the mirrors in the ceiling to whirl. A soft voice sang, "Sleep… sleep…sleep…"

George murmured, "Katherine, I didn't want to come here. You forced me into it. You made me do it. God, I wish I wasn't here. I wish I could go back. I don't want to kill you."

The mirrors glittered as they rotated softly.

He slept.

. . .

He dreamed. He was forty-one again, he and Katie running on a green hill somewhere with a picnic lunch, their helicopter beside them. The wind blew Katie's hair in golden strands and she was laughing. They kissed and held hands, not eating. They read poems; it seemed they were always reading poems.

Other scenes. Quick changes of color, in flight. He and Katie flying over Greece and Italy and Switzerland, in that clear, long autumn of 1997! Flying and never stopping!

And then—nightmare. Katie and Leonard Phelps. George cried out in his sleep. How had it happened? Where had Phelps sprung from? Why had he interfered? Why couldn't life be simple and good? Was it the difference in age? George touching fifty, and Katie so young, not yet twenty-eight? Why, why?

The scene was unforgettably vivid. Leonard Phelps and Katherine in a green park beyond the city. George himself appearing on a path, only in time to see the kissing of their mouths.

The rage. The struggle. The attempt to kill Leonard Phelps.

More days, more nightmares.

George Hill awoke, weeping.

• • •

"Mr. Hill, we're ready for you now."

Hill arose clumsily. He saw himself in the high and now silent mirrors, and he looked all fifty of his years. It had been a wretched error. Better men than he had taken young wives only to have them dissolve away in their hands like sugar crystals under water. He eyed himself, monstrously. A little too much stomach. A little too much chin. Somewhat too much pepper in the hair and not enough in the limbs....

The dark man led him to a room.

George Hill gasped. "This is *Katie's* room!"

"We try to have everything perfect."

"It *is*, to the last detail!"

George Hill drew forth a signed check for ten thousand dollars. The man departed with it.

The room was silent and warm.

George sat and felt for the gun in his pocket. A lot of money. But rich men can afford the luxury of cathartic murder. The violent unviolence. The death without death.

The murder without murdering. He felt better. He was suddenly calm. He watched the door. This was a thing he had anticipated for six months and now it was to be ended. In a moment the beautiful robot, the stringless marionette would appear, and….

. . .

"Hello, George."

"Katie!"

He whirled.

"Katie." He let his breath out.

She stood in the doorway behind him. She was dressed in a feather-soft green gown. On her feet were woven gold-twine sandals. Her hair was bright about her throat and her eyes were blue and clear.

He did not speak for a long while. "You're beautiful," he said at last, shocked.

"How else could I be?"

His voice was slow and unreal. "Let me look at you."

He put out his vague hands like a sleepwalker. His heart pounded sluggishly. He moved forward as if walking under a deep pressure of water. He walked around and around her, touching her.

"Haven't you seen enough of me in all these years?"

"Never enough," he said, and his eyes were filled with tears.

"What did you want to talk to me about?"

"Give me time, please, a little time." He sat down weakly and put his trembling hands to his chest. He blinked. "It's incredible. Another nightmare. How did they *make* you?"

"We're not allowed to talk of that; it spoils the illusion."

"It's magic!"

"Science."

Her touch was warm. Her fingernails were perfect as seashells. There was no seam, no flaw. He looked upon her. He remembered again the words they had read so often in the good days. *Thou art fair, my love. Behold, thou art fair; Thou hast dove's eyes within thy locks. Thy lips are like a spread of scarlet. And thy speech is comely. Thy two breasts are like two young roes that are twins, which feed among the lilies. There is no spot in thee.*

"George?"

"What?" His eyes were cold glass.

He wanted to kiss her lips.

Honey and milk are under thy tongue,
And the smell of thy garments is like the smell of Lebanon.

"George."

A vast humming. The room began to whirl.

"Yes, yes, a moment, a moment." He shook his humming head.

How beautiful are thy feet with shoes, O prince's daughter! The joints of thy thighs are like jewels, the work of the hands of a cunning workman...

"How did they do it?" he cried. In so short a time. Three hours, while he slept. Had they melted gold, fixed delicate watchsprings, diamonds, glitter, confetti, rich rubies, liquid silver, copper thread? Had metal insects spun her hair? Had they poured yellow fire in moulds and set it to freeze?

"No," she said. "If you talk that way, I'll go."

"Don't!"

"Come to business, then," she said, coldly. "You want to talk to me about Leonard."

"Give me time, I'll get to it."

"Now," she insisted.

He knew no anger. It had washed out of him at her appearance. He felt childishly dirty.

"Why did you come to see me?" She was not smiling.

"Please."

"I insist. Wasn't it about Leonard? You know I love him, don't you?"

"Stop it!" He put his hands to his ears.

She kept at him, "You know, I spend all of my time with him now. Where you and I used to go, now Leonard and I stay. Remember the picnic green on Mount Verde? We were there last week. We flew to Athens a month ago, with a case of champagne."

He licked his lips, "You're not guilty, you're *not*." He rose and held her wrists, "You're fresh, you're not *her*. *She's* guilty, not you. You're different!"

"On the contrary," said the woman. "I *am* her, I can act only as she acts. No part of me is alien to her. For all intents and purposes we are one."

"But you did not do what she has done!"

"I did all those things. I kissed him."

"You can't have, you're just born!"

"Out of her past and from your mind."

"Look," he pleaded, shaking her to gain her attention. "Isn't there some way, can't I—pay more money? Take you away with me? We'll go to Paris or Stockholm or any place you like!"

She laughed. "The marionettes only rent. They never sell."

"But I've money!"

"It was tried, long ago. It leads to insanity. It's not possible. Even this much is illegal, you *know* that. We exist only through governmental sufferance."

"All I want is to live with you, Katie."

"That can never be, because I am Katie, every bit of me is her. We do not want competition. Marionettes can't leave the premises; dissection might reveal our secrets. Enough of this.

I warned you, we mustn't speak of these things. You'll spoil the illusion. You'll feel frustrated when you leave. You paid your money, now do what you came to do."

"I don't want to kill you."

"One part of you does. You're walling it in, you're trying not to let it out."

He took the gun from his pocket. "I'm an old fool, I should never have come. You're so beautiful."

"I'm going to see Leonard tonight."

"Don't talk."

"We're flying to Paris in the morning."

"You heard what I said!"

"And then to Stockholm." She laughed sweetly and caressed his chin. "My little fat man."

Something began to stir in him. His face grew pale. He knew what was happening. The hidden anger and revulsion and hatred in him was sending out faint pulses of thoughts. And the delicate telepathic web in her wondrous head was receiving the death thoughts. The marionette. The invisible strings. He himself manipulating her body.

"Plump, odd little man, who once was so fair."

"Don't," he said.

"Old while I am only twenty-seven, ah, George, you were blind, working years to give me time to fall in love again. Don't you think Leonard is lovely?"

He raised the gun blindly.

"Katie."

"His head is as the most fine gold—" she whispered.

"Katie, don't!" he screamed.

"His locks are bushy and black as a raven, his hands are as gold rings set with the beryl!"

How could she speak that song! It was in *his* mind, how could *she* mouth it!

"Katie, don't make me do this!"

"His cheeks are as a bed of spices," she murmured, eyes closed, moving about the room softly. *"His belly is as bright ivory overlaid with sapphires; his legs are as pillars of marble—"*

"Katie!" he shrieked.

"His mouth is most sweet—"

One shot.

"—this is my beloved—"

Another shot.

She fell.

"Katie, Katie, Katie!"

Four more times he pumped bullets into her body.

She lay shuddering. Her senseless mouth clicked wide and some insanely warped mechanism had her repeat again and again, "beloved, beloved, beloved, beloved, beloved…"

George Hill fainted.

PUNISHMENT WITHOUT CRIME

• • •

He awakened to a cool cloth on his brow.

"It's all over," said the dark man.

"Over?" George Hill whispered.

The dark man nodded.

George Hill looked weakly down at his hands. They had been covered with blood. When he fainted he had dropped to the floor. The last thing he remembered was the feeling of the real blood pouring upon his hands in a freshet.

His hands were now clean washed.

"I've got to leave," said George Hill.

"If you feel capable."

"I'm all right." He got up. "I'll go to Paris now, start over. I'm not to try to phone Katie or anything, am I?"

"Katie is dead."

"Yes. I killed her, didn't I? God, the blood, it was *real!*"

"We are proud of that touch."

He went down in the elevator to the street. It was raining and he wanted to walk for hours. The anger and destruction were purged away. The memory was so terrible that he would never wish to kill again. Even if the real Katie were to appear before him now, he would only thank God, and fall senselessly to his knees. She was dead now.

He had had his way. He had broken the law and no one would know.

The rain fell cool on his face. He must leave immediately, while the purge was in effect. After all, what the use of such purges if one took up the old threads? The marionettes' function was primarily to prevent actual crime. If you wanted to kill, hit or torture someone, you took it out on one of those unstrung automatons. It wouldn't do to return to the apartment now. Katie might be there. He wanted only to think of her as dead, a thing attended to in deserving fashion.

He stopped at the curb and watched the traffic flash by. He took deep breaths of the good air and began to relax.

"Mr. Hill?" said a voice at his elbow.

"Yes?"

A manacle was snapped to Hill's wrist. "You're under arrest."

"But—"

"Come along. Smith, take the other men upstairs, make the arrests!"

"You can't do this to me," said George Hill.

"For murder, yes, we can."

Thunder sounded in the sky.

• • •

PUNISHMENT WITHOUT CRIME

It was eight fifteen at night. It had been raining for ten days. It rained now on the prison walls. He put his hands out to feel the drops gather in pools on his trembling palms.

A door clanged and he did not move but stood with his hands in the rain. His lawyer looked up at him on his chair and said, "It's all over. You'll be executed tonight."

George Hill listened to the rain.

"She wasn't real. I didn't kill her."

"It's the law, anyhow. You remember. The others are sentenced, too. The president of Marionettes, Incorporated, will die at midnight. His three assistants will die at one. You'll go about one-thirty."

"Thanks," said George. "You did all you could. I guess it was murder, no matter how you look at it, image or not. The idea was there, the plot and the plan was there. It lacked only the real Katie herself."

"It's a matter of timing, too," said the lawyer. "Ten years ago you wouldn't have got the death penalty. Ten years from now you wouldn't, either. But they had to have an object case, a whipping boy. The use of marionettes has grown so in the last year it's fantastic. The public must be scared out of it, and scared badly. God knows where it would all wind up if it went on. There's the spiritual side of it, too, where does life begin or end, are the robots alive or dead? More than one church has been split up the seams on the question. If they aren't alive, they're the next thing to it, they react, they even think; you know the 'live robot' law that was passed two months ago; you come under that. Just bad timing, is all, bad timing."

"The government's right. I see that now," said George Hill.

"I'm glad you understand the attitude of the law."

"Yes. After all, they can't let murder be legal. Even if it's done with machines and telepathy and wax. They'd be hypocrites to let me get away with my crime. For it *was* a crime. I've felt guilty about it ever since. I've felt the need of punishment. Isn't that odd? That's how society gets to you. It makes you feel guilty even when you see no reason to be…"

"I have to go now. Is there anything you want?"

"Nothing, thanks."

"Good-bye then, Mr. Hill."

The door shut.

• • •

George Hill stood up on the chair, his hands twisting together, wet, outside the window bars. A red light burned in the wall suddenly. A voice came over the audio: "Mr. Hill, your wife is here to see you."

He gripped the bars.

"She's dead," he thought.

"Mr. Hill?" asked the voice.

"She's dead. I killed her."

"Your wife is waiting in the anteroom, will you see her?"

"I saw her fall, I shot her, I saw her fall dead!"

"Mr., Hill, do you hear me?"

"Yes!" he shouted, pounding at the wall with his fists. "I hear you. I hear you! She's dead, she's dead, can't she let me be! I killed her, I won't see her, she's dead!"

A pause. "Very well, Mr. Hill," murmured the voice.

The red light winked off.

Lightning flashed through the sky and lit his face. He pressed his hot cheeks to the cold bars and waited, while the rain fell. After a long time, a door opened somewhere onto the street and he saw two caged figures emerge from the prison office below. They paused under an arc light and glanced up.

It was Katie. And beside her, Leonard Phelps.

"Katie!"

Her face turned away. The man took her arm. They hurried across the avenue in the black rain and got into a low car.

"Katie!" He wrenched at the bars. He screamed and beat and pulled at the concrete ledge. "She's alive! Guard! Guard! I saw her! She's not dead, I didn't kill her, now you can let me out! I didn't murder anyone, it's all a joke, a mistake, I saw her, I saw her! Katie, come back, tell them, Katie, say you're alive! Katie!"

The guards came running.

"You can't kill me! I didn't do anything! Katie's alive, I saw her!"

"We saw her, too, sir."

"But let me free, then! Let me free!" It was insane. He choked and almost fell.

"We've been through all that, sir, at the trial."

"It's not fair!" He leaped up and clawed at the window, bellowing.

The car drove away, Katie and Leonard inside it. Drove away to Paris and Athens and Venice and London next spring and Stockholm next summer and Vienna in the fall.

"Katie, come back, you can't *do* this to me!"

The red tail-light of the car dwindled in the cold rain. Behind him, the guards moved forward to take hold of him while he screamed.

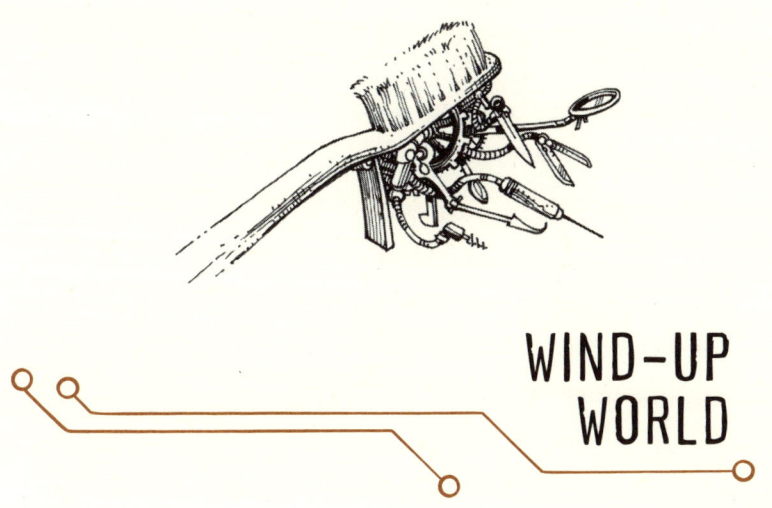

WIND-UP WORLD

Very early in the morning the two men encountered each other on the country road. They both seemed of a mind so they sat facing each other, one on a rail fence, the other against a tree, lamenting as they smoked their cigarettes.

"Name's Hogan," said one.

"Mine's Cabell," said the second.

They nodded seriously, each taking out a cigarette.

"It's a terrible world," said Cabell. "I'm fleeing from the city, or what's left of it, now. I had my feed of it when, one morning, my toothbrush yanked out one of my molars!"

"What won't they invent next," said Hogan, shaking his head.

Cabell nursed his jaw. "I bought that goddamned fiendish device from a machine they nailed on my front door one morning. You remember when they started putting those dispensers on everyone's door, just put a coin in and ask for what you wanted and you got it?"

"I do remember," said Hogan.

"So I buy this toothbrush, an innocent appearing thing, and I'm brushing my teeth with it, when, with a magical eye or some such, the toothbrush suddenly planted itself, gave a grunt, and out, into the porcelain bowl of my bathroom pops my second molar, blood, pip and all!"

"Ah, ah," sighed Hogan.

"I must admit," said Cabell, reluctantly. "The toothbrush *did* fill six cavities, however."

"What do you think of those mailboxes," said Hogan, at last, "that read your letters to you?"

"It wasn't so much the reading I minded," snapped Cabell. "It was when they started writing replies for me!"

"I don't suppose you approve of them beds they invented for when your wife is away from home?" Hogan arched a brow.

"My God! I refuse to *talk* of it!" And Cabell broke his cigarette into a hundred bits. He leaned forward, waving his hand on the air, eyes wide, voice secretive. "Everything not what it seems," he whispered. "That's the trouble. How can a man orient himself, I ask? What's a man to expect if his hat gives his scalp a massage, his ear muffs clean out his ears, and his shoes walk him briskly around the block whether he wants to or not? What would happen, I ask you, if you *sat down* one of them new-fangled cushions!"

"I shudder to think," said Hogan.

"No," announced Cabell. "I'm through with it all, home, cities, towns. Cities are changing, too. They've torn down all the stores and everyone's out of business because you've got everything you need in the home. Everything that's unnecessary is gone. Efficiency, efficiency. I'm off it all, into the country for me, where a tree's a tree, a cow's a cow!"

Hogan said, "You can't win, they'll find you, they'll not let you get away. It's a losing fight. I watched over the years myself, they eliminated roads because, with six sided televisions, four walls, the floor and the roof of your parlor, you could be in New York, Timbuctoo, Ecuador, England. I watched the country jungle kick up the concrete in the roads." He sighed. "And there were no more airplanes for the same reason, you could transact all business without moving. No more cars in the cities because you had a nightclub in your kitchen, a theatre, a park, fresh air, all of it."

"And finally, no more cities," said Cabell. "Just little caps that fitted over the eyes and mouth that fed you, delighted you, played music to your ears, transacted business for you, knew what you thought before you thought it. Who started all this, anyway."

"I don't know," said Hogan.

"And then there was the day they said no more children to my wife," said Cabell. "Not for fifty years. Because we're all going to live to be two hundred years old, with vitamins, and there's no use for children at this time. No more nothing. I'm really afraid of what might happen next. I wonder if they've been working on it. I wonder if they'll do it. Men are unnecessary, you know, too, since the test tube became a father."

"You poor fellow," said Hogan, getting up. "Haven't you *heard?*"

"What?" cried Cabell.

"Ah, I won't tell you," said Hogan. "Good day."

Cabell did not move from where he sat. His eyes were staring white.

Hogan, walking down the road, had a large mechanical key protruding from his back.

MURDER BY FACSIMILE

an outline for a screenplay

GEORGE and KATHERINE HILL have had a perfect marriage, so it has always seemed, though GEORGE HILL is some 15 years older than his wife. They want for nothing, since HILL is an advertising executive whose journeys and talents take him across the world, a fabulous world existing somewhere in the next forty or fifty years.

But then HILL discovers what many a man before him discovers, that riches and talent, in the final sum, are worthless if love falls into disrepair. He begins to suspect that KATHERINE's gaze has strayed to warmer hearths, more vital experiences with younger men. Acting on his intuition, HILL follows his wife and discovers her, beyond town, with LEONARD FELLOWES. He accosts them, and is humiliated when LEONARD FELLOWES, attacked, easily puts him down, forces him to his knees, with his superior strength. His pride further destroyed in the presence of KATHERINE, HILL can only weep and cry out with frustration as FELLOWES takes her away into the sky, in a helicopter, to the far ends of the earth. "I'll find you!" HILL shouts. "No matter where you go! And kill you, kill you both!" But we know he is frustrated, and the threat is useless, as his love is borne away into the clouds.

• • •

A few days later, GEORGE HILL receives an envelope by special delivery. It is a letter of advertisement from FACSIMILE LTD, noting that he is needful of their help, and advising him to visit their offices at the most convenient hour. The letter, exposed to the air for sixty seconds, dissolves into snowflakes, destroys itself on the carpet. FACSIMILE LTD, we are given to understand is a clandestine company, outlawed by federal statute. All evidence, such as this advertisement, is prepared so as to be self-destructive, from chemical compounds baked into the material.

HILL goes to the FACSIMILE LTD offices, where he provides them with a detailed description of his wife, a lock of her hair, some of her old party dresses, and perfumes. He signs a check for a large amount, and puts himself into a slumber room to await the arrival of his wife, KATHERINE. She does arrive, of course, paid for, and manufactured as a robot device, a perfect facsimile of the real woman, by FACSIMILE LTD.

Everything about the mechanical woman is so absolutely realized that as HILL talks with her, deluded, he forgets her electronic derivation, and tries to persuade her to come back to him, go home at last, forget the past. It is up to the robot to remind him that she is not flesh, but only a 'fantoccini,' a shadow-show-puppet, and is here to provide an outlet for his frustrated passion to murder. So murder he must, to benefit from his investment. When he refuses to 'kill' her, thus harmlessly channeling his violence toward a robot instead of a human, the robot resourcefully taunts him. She reminds him of her 'love' for Leonard, and so enrages HILL once more that, at last, he does the deed. He shoots and kills the facsimile KATHERINE. He weeps by her destroyed body. At last, though the real Katherine is off somewhere around the world, he has caught up with her and paid her back for his ruined pride and spoiled life.

• • •

In the street, in the rain, HILL discovers a terrible, a strange, an unexpected thing—he feels guilt. Even though the creature he has destroyed is not real, is only a machine, she was so much like Katherine that now he is riven with anguish and remorse. He goes into a church to confess his strange sin, to ask forgiveness for killing a machine. THE FATHER who hears his confession, troubled, can offer no advice, nothing immediate that is, for this is a new situation in a technological society of many new surprises.

Coming from the church, HILL is arrested by the Federal Police.

He greets them almost with relief. He has need for punishment. He asks to be punished. He has done a terrible thing.

• • •

The Court agrees with HILL. He must be punished. In reaction to the onslaught of mechanical robot life that has infiltrated society on every level, in politics, in business, in sex, the Federal Government has recently passed a law exacting the death penalty for anyone found guilty of using a robot device, shaped like man, woman, or child, for 'facsimile murder.' Ten years earlier, such 'murders' and such a law might have been unknown, were unknown. Ten years from this day, the law might be modified, as psychologists saw the use and need of such machines in our society to help man vent his rages and passions on harmless objects in order to become more 'human' himself, the rest of the time. The robots, some day, might well be the solution to man half-ape and half-human, and his way to being an angel but always tripped flat by the demon destruction in his breast. HILL, caught in a time between an age of ignorance and a dawn of enlightenment, must be sacrificed to society's present need, to destroy, in turn, what it does not as yet understand.

HILL is sentenced to be executed.

• • •

On the night of his execution, HILL is startled to hear that KATHERINE has asked to come visit him. She has come back from the Orient to see him, to commiserate with him, to see if she can help, but there is nothing she can do. At first, HILL refuses to see her, but then, needing to be released from his guilt at her 'facsimile murder' admits her to his cell. There, incredulous, he sees her alive, and feels the dread weight of conscience fall from his shoulders. She is alive, alive! He is guilty of nothing. So…call off the execution! Here, this woman is PROOF he has done nothing! Guards! Guards! But the hour is up. The lawyer enters. KATHERINE leaves. It is time for GEORGE HILL to die. He is *not* innocent. He *did* destroy, if only a shadow, an image, of a woman. The dark seed was in his mind. GEORGE leaps to the window to shout down into the rain: 'Kate, come back! Tell them you're alive! Save me! I'm innocent! I'm innocent! I've done nothing! Katie, Kate!" And he sees her drive off in the rain, with LEONARD FELLOWES, as the Guards take hold of him and move him steadily through a door into a room where the Chair waits, and the door...*slams!*